A Bad Apple

Also by Alice Zogg

Stand-Alone Mysteries
Exposing the Past
No Curtain Call
The Ill-Fated Scientist
Accidental Eyewitness
A Bet Turned Deadly

R. A. Huber Mysteries
Evil at Shore Haven
Guilty or Not
Murder at the Cubbyhole
Revamp Camp
Final Stop Albuquerque
The Fall of Optimum House
The Lonesome Autocrat
Tracking Backward
Turn the Joker Around
Reaching Checkmate

A Bad Apple

ALICE ZOGG

aventine press

This book is a work of fiction.

Published by Aventine Press
55 East Emerson St.
Chula Vista CA 91911
www.aventinepress.com

ISBN: 978-1-59330-997-8

Library of Congress Control Number: 2021913134
Library of Congress Cataloging-in-Publication Data
A Bad Apple/Alice Zogg
Printed in the United States of America

In memory of Gustav

CREDITS

Thanks are in order to Mary Froede, who helped with my research about the garment industry. She answered all my questions, and then some. My daughter came to the rescue again with her proofreading skills. I do not take you for granted, Franziska! My gratitude goes out to Gayle Bartos-Pool for her excellent editing. As always, she was spot-on. Last, but not least, I thank my husband, Wilfried, for being the steady calm in my life. For several months during the pandemic I avoided writing. With all the worry preoccupying my mind, I was unable to have a creative thought. It was due to his serene example that I at last pulled myself together and started to plot ideas for this book, first in my mind, then putting them on the page.

CAST OF CHARACTERS

Cecile Long-Horton   Owner and CEO of Basic Wrappers; has control over her company

Bruce Horton   Cecile's husband; a department store buyer, recently furloughed

Jason Long   Cecile's oldest son; the CFO of Basic Wrappers

Candy Long   Jason's wife; a stay-at-home mom with an optimistic outlook on life

Darrell Long   Cecile's other son; the CIO of Basic Wrappers

Sybille Long   Darrell's wife; an ambitious pharmaceutical sales representative

Julie Martinez   Cecile's daughter; in charge of Basic Wrappers' employees

Mateo Martinez   Julie's husband; works for a heating and air-conditioning outfit

Carole Pedrotti   Bruce's high school girlfriend; a grocery store manager

Antonia Silva   The Hortons' housekeeper; has worked 10 years for them

Raul Ibarra   The Hortons' gardener; has taken good care of their yard

Lt. Claudia Campbell   Officer of the Monrovia City Police Department in charge of the case

Sprint   Detective Campbell's colleague

Eduard Blyte   Partner at the law offices of Stolzerman, Blyte & Morales

Dr. Norma Wong   Cecile's oncologist

CHAPTER 1

The board of directors' meeting of Basic Wrappers held via Zoom at the end of August in 2020 was in full swing. Cecile Long-Horton, owner and CEO of the corporation had called it to order and heated arguments soon ensued. Even though the gathering was only virtual, the dispute was no less fierce.

Jason, her oldest son and CFO, moved his face closer to the camera and stressed, "Producing face masks and giving them away for free was a nice gesture at the beginning of the pandemic, but Mom, you know good and well that we can no longer afford to do so. If no substantial money comes in soon, we'll be operating in the red!"

Cecile's other son, Darrell, the company's CIO, jumped in, saying, "I'm sure that I don't need to remind everyone that our clientele consists of restaurant owners, hair salons, and customers ordering Halloween costumes and outfits for special occasions. Covid-19 practically put the first two out of business, and who wants to have anything to do with dress-up parties of any kind in the current situation? The only thing that's a hot sell right now are face masks, and we're giving them away!"

Cecile, who had always led her company with an iron fist, stayed firm and said, "Most businesses are suffering, ours included, but I will not take advantage of the less fortunate during this time of their urgent need. We will keep offering the masks for free. Basic Wrappers will manage and survive."

The CEO's daughter, Julie Martinez, who had been silent thus far, spoke up. "At first, when masks were scarce, it made total sense to give them away. It kept our seamstresses and other employees busy, as orders from clients became limited, but now disposable masks are readily available and cheap. Nobody needs to rely on getting cloth masks any longer."

Cecile shot back, "They're not cheap for the homeless and poor people. And who among them could keep a steady supply, since they're only worn once and then discarded? No, I'm staying firm in my decision: The masks we produce are free of charge."

Darrell raised both arms and shouted, "How do you propose we can stay above water? We are more than five months into the pandemic and it doesn't look like there's an end to it soon. We have practically no new orders. Our only steady source of income would be the masks, should we start selling them. We could even make a nice profit if we were to turn out fashion and sports team masks."

Jason said, "I agree. It looks like the masks are here to stay for a long time. Why not profit from them? We could use a little profit rather than keep operating at a loss."

Not blinking an eye, their mother stated, "You heard me; the masks are and will be free for the duration. I tell you how it's done. We tighten our belts. I, for one, am not drawing any money out of the company until our troubles are over. If necessary, I'll help the corporation out of my own pocket. And I suggest that we cut all of your salaries down by half."

That announcement silenced her adult children and left them staring open-mouthed into their respective cameras.

She looked over to Jason's Zoom square and asked, "How much profit did we make last year?"

"I would have to look up the figure," he stammered.

"No need. I am positive that it was substantial. We can draw from that profit to sustain us for right now. If the pandemic continues for many more months, we'll all tighten our belts, like I said."

Julie questioned the CEO, "You told me not to furlough any of the employees. How can I keep all our staff busy? Sewing only masks isn't going to do it and most of our outstanding orders are filled."

"Get creative! You could design patriotic flags people can attach to the sides of their cars. After all, we are in an election year. Since you're also in charge of advertising, offer people either red ones or blue ones, depending on their choice of political party. And if undecided, they can attach one of each to the sides of their vehicles."

Darrell saw the humor in her last remark and could not suppress a grin.

Ready to end the board meeting, Cecile Long-Horton announced out of the blue: "There is a bad apple among us." And pointing a finger straight at the camera she added, "You know who you are. It needs to stop! I'm keeping an eye on you."

That said, she adjourned the meeting.

CHAPTER 2

Bruce Horton, Cecile's second husband, had entered the study of their home in Monrovia, California, in time to overhear part of the board's dispute and the accusation his wife hurled at her offspring before she adjourned the meeting.

He said, "Sorry I butted in on your meeting. I keep forgetting that you've turned the study into your office."

"No problem."

"I'm curious, though. Which one is the 'bad apple'?"

"I'd rather not say."

He knew better than to press her further. This was between her and one of her kids. Cecile could be aloof at times, but there was one thing he realized after ten years of marriage: she stayed firm in her decisions. She now turned back to her computer and the subject was closed.

Bruce watched her as she concentrated on her screen, seeming to do research. At 69, she was still a good-looking woman. Her face showed some signs of aging, but her blue eyes were steady and clear. He was not sure if she colored her hair; it had remained the same shade of ash blonde for a decade. She only changed its style now and then. Best of all, she had kept her youthful figure.

He mused, Cecile had definitely been a good catch even if she was 11 years his senior. From the beginning he had made no secret of the fact that he hated his job as buyer of a major department store and was looking to retire early. The idea was for him to stick it through until his 60th birthday in two years, but now he was furloughed, thanks to Covid-19, and had to apply for unemployment benefits. He always figured that Cecile would continue working and his comfortable lifestyle would be secured. At the moment he was not so sure. He knew practically nothing of her company, only the very minimum she had been willing to share.

She suddenly turned to him and asked, "Is there something on your mind?"

He replied, "Your business is going to survive, right?"

"Of course."

"Even if the pandemic goes on for many more months?"

"Basic Wrappers' profits have been substantial in recent years, so it should be able to withstand the current crisis. If not, I have enough personal capital to pitch in."

"That's a relief!"

Then she said, "Do you mind? I have a personal phone call to make," and he left her to it.

CHAPTER 3

With his hands shaking and grey eyes barely focused, Jason Long had vanished into the master bathroom at his residence in Sierra Madre, immediately after the board of directors' meeting was adjourned. The trouble with working from home was that it did not allow him any privacy. At the office, he had his own domain, and if he closed the door, no employee would enter without knocking. Here, the wife and kids dropped in and out as they pleased. Sure, he had established a makeshift office in the den, and the kids did their online schooling in their bedrooms, but after all, it was their den too.

He came out of the bathroom not quite as angry and with his nerves more under control, finding his wife, Candy, in the kitchen preparing lunch. Candy was the girl-next-door type and a stay-at-home mom. The dark-brown, short, curly hair framed her face and the sparkle in her eyes reflected a great sense of humor with an optimistic outlook on life.

Taking one look at her spouse, she inquired, "What's wrong?"

"Mom is what's wrong. She is stubborn as a mule! Basic Wrappers is going to fold, thanks to her. You'll see." And he told her about the disagreement that had evolved at the meeting and the CEO's demand of cutting their salaries in half. "Can you imagine, a cut of 50 percent! She put it out as a so called suggestion, but we all know that it's an order."

Candy said, "It's not the end of the world. We can manage with less money for a while."

"You're taking her side? Unbelievable!"

"I'm not, but just reassuring you that we will be okay. It stands to reason that we are spending less anyway, due to Covid-19. Not going out to dinner, making hardly any purchases other than necessities, and cancelling our summer vacation to Europe this year, is saving us tons of money."

As if he hadn't heard her argument, he continued, "And what's more, she accused one of us of some wrongdoing."

"I don't understand."

"The way she put it was that one of us is a bad apple."

"What on earth does she mean?"

"I have no idea."

At that point, eleven-year-old Mike and nine-year-old Sophia, followed by Bigfoot, their lab, came blowing in like a whirlwind, asking, "What's for lunch?"

"Grilled cheese sandwiches. Go wash your hands," their mom replied.

Jason thought, what if she meant me with her "bad apple" statement?

CHAPTER 4

For a second Cecile's mind lingered on the private phone conversation she had just had with her daughter. Whether or not her reprimand did any good remained to be seen. Then she mulled over the topic at the board of directors' meeting once more and had to acknowledge that her kids were spoiled brats. The world around them grew daily with more virus cases, police brutalities, Black Lives Matter protests, and now the numerous brush fires, but her selfish children were only concerned with filling their own pockets. They had no idea about financial hardship. Their jobs were practically handed to them the minute they got out of college.

She could not help but reminisce about the early days of Basic Wrappers. Widowed 40 years ago at age 29, with three young children to take care of, she had to find a way to make a living. She had been well aware of the danger involved when marrying John, a professional car racer, but took her chances. The tragedy happened; he spun out in a curve, flipped multiple times, landed up-side-down and was killed instantly. She had used a portion of the life insurance he left her to start and later to further the business, and put the rest in a college fund for her kids. For the first few years of Basic Wrappers, she did her own sewing at home while taking care of her young family.

She smiled at her recollection of the beginning, when she started out making aprons in floral and printed calicos, deciding to market them by exhibiting in various food shows. By word of mouth, her apron line was soon featured in major department stores all over the country. She had to hustle to get the orders filled, keeping her sewing machine rattling long after tucking her small charge in bed. When she got orders from restaurant chains, not only for aprons but also place mats and tablecloths made from vinyl or fabric, it was time to hire a contractor to help with the cutting and sewing at his house. At that point, she went wholesale with the mills that created the fabrics she used, driving to downtown L. A. to their locations to pick up the material she needed.

Basic Wrappers got even bigger, as uniforms were added to the orders of restaurant chains. She had also extended the production by supplying hair cutting capes to beauty salons, and getting custom orders for Halloween costumes and outfits for other occasions. She attributed her success to the fact that her creations were made in the USA, and that she gave excellent service. By the time her firstborn became a teen, the company had outgrown the in-house production and needed its own location.

And here is where the bulk of the life insurance money came into play. Cecile remembered how she contacted a real estate company to show her industrial spaces for a warehouse, production, and office, all in one place. She settled for a property in El Monte, north of the 10 Freeway on Peck Road. The location was ideal: low rent and near the workers market, and most important, not far from her home in Monrovia. She also saw potential for growth. If necessary, the property had plenty of room for additions to be built in the future.

Basic Wrappers had always been her top priority, and only ten years ago, when Bruce came along, did she finally allow herself to have a private life. By that time her sons and daughter had long come on board and the business had been turned into a corporation, with her in command and each of her kids holding a position.

She sighed and thought, I've worked hard for four decades to get where we are today. The current state of the world isn't going to ruin us. And now is the time to show some compassion for the less fortunate.

CHAPTER 5

Unlike her mom and brothers, Julie did not work from home during the pandemic. As manager of Basic Wrappers' workforce, she was present at the El Monte plant. A fair and compassionate boss, her employees respected and appreciated her. Everyone was extremely careful during the current situation and, so far, no one had come down with the virus. On that Friday, August 28, Julie immersed herself wholeheartedly into her job, trying not to dwell on the Zoom board meeting of that morning, nor that phone conversation she'd had with her mother thereafter.

Now, at the end of the workday, with the rattling of sewing machines having come to a stop and the last of the seamstresses heading out the door, saying, "*Buenas noches, señora Martinez, nos vemos el lunes,*" she had the place to herself.

She surveyed her domain. They had made some required adjustments to the place. The sewing machine stations had been re-organized to a distance of six feet apart from each other, and the 25-foot-long cutting table had been moved to the edge of the large room, as far away from the stations as possible. Spaced out at the far end of the area, her office cubicle was surrounded by translucent plastic shields.

A connecting door led to a large area for storage of unused fabric, vinyl, and completed items. Adjacent to the huge production section of the building, there was a kitchen with a sink, refrigerator, microwave, and tables with chairs. Workers rarely sat down in it nowadays, preferring to take their lunches outdoors to the benches in the yard behind the plant.

The second floor housed the offices of her mom and brothers, plus a conference room, all of which had not been in use for months. As a matter of fact, the door leading to the stairs to get up there was locked now. Julie, as manager, had the key to it. As far back as the spring, she had made it her habit to sneak up to the conference room for some private time during her lunchbreak hour.

She made a last inspection of the plant, making sure all the machines and irons were turned off, set the air conditioner to weekend mode, then pressed the light switches and locked up.

On the drive home to Duarte, she could not avoid mulling over what had transpired at the meeting, and the more she thought about her mother's call immediately afterwards, the angrier she got. By the time she reached her house, she was fuming.

CHAPTER 6

Mateo Martinez beat his wife home by a few minutes. He worked for a heating-and-air-conditioning outfit and his job was secured. People's A/C's broke down regardless of a pandemic. Friday nights used to be "date night," which was no longer on their agenda these days. One look at Julie when she stormed in the door was enough to know that she didn't feel like cooking.

"Want me to call for pizza delivery?" he asked.

"Whatever! I'm not hungry."

"You can't be mad at me," he joked, "I haven't done anything, as far as I can remember."

She did not answer and brushed by him on her way to the master bedroom to change into a comfortable house dress and slippers.

Forty-five minutes later, having consumed the pizza and lingering in the dining room over a glass of Pinot Noir, Julie finally told her husband all about the debate at that morning's meeting.

Mateo heard her out and then said, "We can manage with your salary cut; my income isn't going to change. We can still pay for Michelle's college education, if that's what's worrying you."

"That's not the point," she shot back. "Basic Wrappers may not survive."

She slapped the table with the palm of her hand, making the wine glasses jump and mimicked her mother's pitch, "'*Get creative!*' Easy for her to say."

"What did she mean with her other remark?"

"Oh, the 'bad apple' thing?" Julie shrugged her shoulders and stated, "I have no idea who and what she meant."

After a long pause Mateo said, "That's not all you are enraged about, is it?"

"No, it's not. Mom called me after the Zoom meeting and got on my case."

"About what?"

"My weight. Oh, how I hate her! So I'm 20 pounds heavier than the charts suggest - - maybe more like 30 by now - - but that's none of her damned business. I don't even understand how she could tell that I'm heavier with only half of our bodies showing on Zoom."

She took a breath and continued, "Not a word like, 'How is Michelle settling in as a freshman?' Or, 'I'm really worried about her exposure to Covid-19 in the dorm.' For a grandmother, that would be a normal topic to have a phone conversation about. After all, our baby is on the east coast, far away from home, during this horrible time. But no, she called to let me know that she was concerned about my weight gain. She said she was being anxious for my health. You and I both know that's a pretext; she wants me to look good."

"There is nothing wrong with the way you look," he put in.

"Agreed, but not in her eyes. She lectured me on the dangers of overeating from stress. She gave me tips on low-carb diets and exercise routines on YouTube that she wanted me to try, and then followed it all up with an e-mail adding both links. I deleted the e-mail without bothering to check out the links."

Julie came up for air again and repeated, "I hate her! She is the most controlled eater I know and keeps to a rigid exercise program. I bet that now, with the gyms closed, she purchased her own workout machines. Mom has no understanding for anyone who doesn't share her enthusiasm for fitness."

Mateo got up from the table, planted himself behind her, began massaging her shoulders and neck, and said, "I love you the way you are." With a smirk he added, "And your cooking is first-rate!"

Her good humor restored for the time being, she remarked, "Thanks to your mom's recipes from her hometown of Oaxaca, Mexico. And you, Mateo, deserve credit for calming me down, as usual."

As they carried their empty glasses over to the kitchen sink, she glanced at his trim body and commented, "Too bad I don't have your metabolism which allows you to eat all the fattening food you want without it showing."

CHAPTER 7

Meanwhile, there was an after-dinner conversation, or rather, a shouting match evolving at Darrell and Sybille Long's residence in San Marino. Like all other officers of Basic Wrappers and its manager, Darrell lived in the San Gabriel Valley, close to their business location in El Monte. However, Darrell and Sybille were the only ones living beyond their means. They opted not to have children and enjoyed life to the fullest, or so it seemed. Sybille was a sales representative for a pharmaceutical firm and planned to continue climbing the ladder.

She now screeched, "Cutting your income in half! The woman is out of her mind and needs to be stopped."

"I don't get it either. And giving away the masks for free at this point is suicide for the company. Mom has always been a shrewd businesswoman. The pandemic is making her soft. But there's nothing we can do about it. She's still the owner of the corporation."

"The woman is 70, for crying out loud! It's past time for her to retire."

"She's actually only 69."

"Same difference. How long is she planning to queen it over Basic Wrappers?"

"Maybe another decade; who knows?"

"Like I said, she needs to be stopped. In the meantime, what do we do?"

Darrell stated, "As CIO I have to balance the best interests of the company and those of the employees."

"Come off your high horse. Our own interests are at stake, and you know it. So what do you suggest?"

"We may have to let go of a few things, like the yacht and the Big Bear cabin, for example."

"What if your precious business goes under?"

"In that case we'd have to sell the house and look for a place that we can afford with only your salary."

"Over my dead body!" she shouted. "I'm not handing over my money. You'd gamble it all away."

He stared at her, stunned.

The antique Biedermeier wall clock struck eight, but they paid no attention and time seemed to stand still while they held each other's glare.

Recovering, Darrell asked, "How long have you known?"

"Did you really think you could hide your gambling addiction from me? I had my suspicions but couldn't be sure. It wasn't just Vegas. You took your golf clubs along on numerous trips to Palm Springs and other locations with Indian casinos, but playing golf was never on your agenda, right? And earlier in the pandemic, during the 11 weeks of total shutdown, you couldn't help yourself and resorted to driving to those sleazy, illegal gambling halls."

"You spied on me?"

"I was curious and worried where you could be going when everything was closed. So I followed you one night."

There was another long silence before Sybille said, "Get help. I'm sure that there is a gamblers anonymous group. But getting back to the subject of your mommy dearest CEO, you and your siblings need to do something about her before she ruins the company and all of us. If you don't, I will!"

Then a smirk came over her lips as she asked, "Could she have meant *you* with your gambling being the bad apple?"

"Beats me!" he replied, throwing his arms up in the air. "I didn't think she knew about it, but then, I had no idea that you did either."

***

Darrell lay awake that night, brooding. Did he really need help like Sybille had suggested? Surely he could overcome the little problem on his own. If it was even a problem, which he was unwilling to admit to himself. So far, win or lose, he was always able to walk away from the tables. In a way he was glad that she knew about the gambling; no more sneaking behind her back. Then his mind dwelled on the rest of the arguments the two of them had had. As always, Sybille was sure of herself and opinionated. He wondered, what did she mean by saying that he and his siblings needed to do something about Mom, and if not, she would?

There had never been any love lost between his wife and her mother-in-law. Now, 18 years later, Mom's words spoken before he married Sybille came to mind. She had said, "Are you sure that you want to spend your life with a high maintenance, self-serving, and pushy sort of a woman?"

He mused, all true. Those were Sybille's traits, but he had been mad about her, and still was. Looking into her big brown eyes and shutting down the mocking smile on her lips with a kiss still gave him a thrill. Then he mulled over the financial strain that lay ahead. If worse came to worse, his wife had made it clear that she wasn't willing to support them both.

What other option was there? In these tough times, he wouldn't be able to find a new position. He had always worked for his mom and couldn't imagine having to create a résumé and go for job interviews. In a flash it hit him, *I may have to resort to extremely high bets in my poker games. After all, life is but a gamble.* And he knew with sudden certainty that he was going to strike it big, one way or another.

Finally at peace, he fell asleep instantly.

CHAPTER 8

Three days later, on Monday, August 31, Bruce, clad in running shorts, stuck his head through the study door and told his wife he was off for a jog in the park.

"Don't forget to put on your mask when coming back into the house. Antonia will be here," Cecile said, and waved to him before turning her attention back to the big screen, where she was following an exercise routine on You Tube.

Antonia Silva was their housekeeper, who had cleaned their Monrovia home every Monday for the last decade. She also chipped in with cooking every so often and helped out when they had guests. During the complete lockdown, Cecile had resorted to being her own homemaker, but she was thankful that Antonia did not shy away from coming back after the restrictions were lifted. They were extremely careful, though, keeping their six feet distance. Other than the housekeeper, nobody besides her and Bruce had entered their home since March. Neither the gardener nor the pool service man had reason to step inside, pandemic or not.

As for being extra careful, Cecile knew that she was at high risk, not just due to her age, but also because of having had breast cancer two years earlier. She hardly had left her house in the last five months, other than for necessities and an occasional stroll around the neighborhood. The one exception had been at the very beginning of the pandemic when she delivered the masks personally, which she felt had justified putting herself at risk. Like most people during the current crisis, she kept Amazon busy and even had her groceries delivered.

Thank God her place was comfortable and she and Bruce could enjoy a dip in the pool to relax. She had lived in the same two-story, four-bedroom house ever since Julie, her youngest, turned two and had seen no reason to move anywhere else as her business became profitable. The home was remodeled a couple of times with a state-of-the-art kitchen, and an addition was constructed onto the master bathroom to accommodate a walk-in Jacuzzi. When her kids were primary-school age, she had a pool built in the backyard, which had been enjoyed by all for many years. After her marriage to Bruce, he converted one of the bedrooms into a billiards room.

As Cecile turned off the TV and walked up the stairs to the master bedroom to change out of her workout clothes, she thought, I've had many housekeepers before but none had been as dear to me as Antonia. She's like a breath of fresh air. Always ready with a quick smile, she's not only extremely competent but seems to enjoy her job. More often than not, the woman is singing while she works. Nowadays, restricted by having her mouth and nose covered, she resorts to humming. Our housekeeper is definitely a jewel, she mused.

Antonia was well-paid, but Cecile had decided to do more. Only in her early forties, Brazilian-born Antonia would most likely outlive both herself and Bruce. That was why, regardless if the woman would still be in their employ or not, Cecile had recently added a legacy to her will benefiting Antonia. Yes, she nodded to herself, I made the right decision.

CHAPTER 9

Bruce was jogging along the trail at his Monrovia neighborhood park as he always did three times a week. He hardly ever encountered people on his early morning runs. An occasional squirrel or rabbit was more likely. His legs kept a steady pace regardless of the path's up or downhill grade, while his mind was preoccupied elsewhere. He had been content and life had been good - - still was - - with Cecile. If only he had not attended his class reunion last September. Since Cecile hadn't wanted to accompany him, he had gone to the event alone. To his downfall, so had Carole Pedrotti. The popular beauty had aged, but her ability to cast a spell on him was still evident from the moment they had made eye contact clear across the room.

He slowed down a tad when he reached a woodsy area and thought, when Carole dumped me for the star football player back in high school, I was crushed. It took me a long time to get over her, but in due course I did. And now she is back in my life once more. Unbelievable, that the woman is still able to bewitch me after all this time!

On the night of the reunion, the two of them caravanned to a Starbucks where they talked at length, catching up. He told her about his first marriage ending in disaster and briefly touched on his present life with Cecile. She, in turn, shared facts about her failed two nuptials and that she had gone back to using her maiden name. They ended up at her place and he hadn't been able to resist her. Again, he was wax in her hands from that night onward. Their affair had gone on for six months when Covid-19 hit.

He was now coming out of the thicket of deciduous trees and paused at the clearing. A few yards below were the picnic tables overlooking the playground, which was deserted. Like all other park play areas in Southern California, it was cordoned off with yellow tape. A lonely figure sat at one of the tables. Bruce donned his mask and walked toward it. He knew what he needed to do but was by no means looking forward to it.

She turned her head, then jumped up, and before she could run into his arms, he stopped her, saying, "We need to keep the six foot distance. Please put on your mask."

She stared. Then said, "You're kidding and must be wearing yours as a joke."

"I'm dead serious."

Realizing she had not brought one along, he reached into his shirt pocket and handed her a spare. Then he made a point of sitting down at the opposite end of the bench from her.

Brushing aside strands of wavy, auburn hair and adjusting the facemask over her ears, she burst out, "You're being ridiculous. First you refused to see me for months, and now we resort to meeting in the park like a couple of teenagers. With your text summoning me here, I certainly didn't think you'd insist on social distancing, or I wouldn't have gotten up at the crack of dawn for this!"

"Be reasonable," he begged. "As a grocery store manager, you're prone to being exposed to Covid-19 on a regular basis."

"We can't all be privileged people, working from home."

"You're taking this the wrong way. What you workers on the front line are doing is heroic but you've got to admit that you are more susceptible to the corona virus than the average person."

"What's the matter with you, anyhow?" she shot back. "Neither one of us is sick with any virus, so what's the big deal?"

"We could be carriers."

"Well, I'm willing to take the gamble. Try to get away tonight after my shift."

It took all his willpower to resist the offer but he said, "I can't take the risk for Cecile's sake. She's in the most vulnerable age group and has a pre-existing condition."

Carole stamped her foot and yelled, "It's always about her! You need to make your choice."

"You know I'm crazy about you."

"Then divorce her!"

"She's my bread and butter."

Carole placed her hands on her hips and asked, "What exactly do you mean by that?"

"I got furloughed," he replied.

"So? She's the one with the big bucks and will have to pay you alimony."

"We have a prenuptial agreement."

There was silence between them as each dealt with his and her own thoughts.

Then she spit out the words, "So this is good-bye?"

He turned to her with pleading eyes. "No! Hold out a little longer. There will be an end to the pandemic and we'll find a solution."

He left her sitting there and jogged all the way home, thinking, I handled this poorly but at this point can't take a chance.

Have I just been stood up? Carole wondered. Her Italian temper flaring, she got up from the bench and kicked it. I may have to resort to drastic action, she mused, and walked to where her car was parked.

CHAPTER 10

In the afternoon on September 15, Darrell asked his siblings for a Zoom session and first inquired if everyone was okay after the recent threat of the *Bobcat* wildfire raging in the nearby Angeles Forest Mountains. Everyone agreed that other than the extremely bad air quality, making them cough in spite of staying indoors with the windows closed, they had come to no harm.

Julie said, "I'm sure you all talked to Mom and know that she and Bruce were packed and ready to evacuate, but thankfully it didn't come to that."

"Speaking of Mom," Jason stated, "I don't like that we have this meeting behind her back. I bet Sybille put you up to the idea, Darrell."

His brother admitted, "It so happens that she did suggest it, but I agree with her that we need to stick our heads together and find a way to stop Mom. We can't allow her to cut our salaries in half. There's got to be a better solution. So Jason, I'm sure you've long done the math. Can Basic Wrappers survive the pandemic?"

"Depends on how much longer it'll last. The so-called experts predict a bad winter ahead, so we're looking well into next year."

"Bottom line?"

"True, we've had a few profitable years before the current crisis hit and have been able to get by so far, like Mom stated, but it won't last much longer. And by the way, she wasn't bluffing with her claim of not taking any money out of the company. She hasn't paid herself a single dime for months. Although I know nothing of her personal finances - - she has her own accountant - - I suspect that she and Bruce can live well drawing from her private capital. Our mother has always been frugal and it serves her well now. You can't blame her for expecting us to also *tighten our belts*, using her words."

Darrell said, "How about applying for a loan?"

"Even if we'd get approved - - and that is iffy at best - - Mom would never go for it. She has the old-fashioned conviction to never, ever run up any debt." He forced a grin and added, "She could teach our politicians a thing or two with respect to the deficit."

Nobody was in the mood to laugh at his joke.

"We may have to resort to furloughing some of the workers." Darrell suggested.

Julie jumped into the conversation by saying, "That's out of the question. We can't do that to them. Besides, Mom would never agree to lay them off."

Darrell pointed at Jason's Zoom square and said, "You have the most clout with Mom. Talk her into letting us charge people for the face masks. Like I tried to make her understand, they could be profitable if we were to turn out fashion and sports team masks. I have plenty of ideas of how they could be marketed to the general public. I guarantee they would sell like hot cakes!"

"We all know that she is firm on that issue. Basic Wrappers masks will always be free."

"For crying out loud! Don't we have a voice? There are three of us against her one opinion!"

"Ah, but she calls the shots. She's the sole owner of the company. Let's face it, we're not partners but only well-paid employees."

"And soon not so well-paid," Darrell remarked.

"I don't like it either," his brother shot back, "but we have to be realistic. Even with a 50 percent cut, our income is still higher than that of the average working American."

"That doesn't change the fact that I can't afford the cut," Darrell yelled.

"You'll have to make adjustments to your lifestyle. Who knows, it may be good for Sybille to come down from her high maintenance pedestal. I've had time to think about Mom's proposal and have come to the conclusion that we all have to make changes to our standard of living and learn to deal with a more frugal approach. Like I said, I'm not thrilled about it, but we can't let the business go under."

Julie chimed in, "A lot of people have lost their jobs and would be happy to trade their situation with ours. Unfortunately, we cannot change Mom, so we have no choice but to go along with having our salaries reduced."

Darrell burst out, "She's ruining the company and all our lives and needs to be stopped! Who has the balls to do it?"

"Don't be so melodramatic. You're giving me a headache and it's time to end this session," Jason replied and promptly hung up, giving the other two no choice but to do likewise.

Julie stared at the dark computer screen and thought, interesting how we all avoided mentioning the "bad apple" thing Mom made a point of mentioning. Surely it must be on everyone's mind. Could it be that she somehow found out about my naughty secret?

CHAPTER 11

Jason had held it together during the Zoom meeting, appearing calm and collected. Now, he rushed out of the den, shaking. In the master bathroom he popped two pills into his mouth, washing them down with a few sips of water. Then he glanced at his image in the mirror and was appalled at the haggard, nervous wreck staring back. An involuntary shriek escaped him as he sat down on the closed toilet seat and shut his eyes.

Minutes later, he returned to the den, refreshed and ready to do some work. Candy stood by the sofa, folding clothes she had retrieved from the dryer.

"Feeling better?" she asked.

"What do you mean?"

"I know your secret."

"What secret?"

She left the unfolded laundry in a heap and walked over toward his desk. Then she touched his shoulder lightly and stated, "I know about your opioid addiction."

His first reaction was anger, which was immediately replaced by relief. Then his glance went to the open door.

"The kids are done with their homework and are watching a movie in Mike's room. We can talk undisturbed," Candy said.

"Have you known for long?"

"A while. I was hoping you'd confide in me."

"It's not that simple. I haven't admitted it even to myself."

In the brief silence that followed she went back to her laundry and started folding again. It seemed easier to continue this conversation while she kept her hands busy.

She asked, "It started last Christmas season after you pulled something in your back while putting up the outdoor lights, right?"

"Correct. I needed a strong pain killer. And before I knew what was happening, I was dependent on the cursed pills. I somehow managed it better and was more in control when I worked at the office during the first three months of the year. Working from home made everything worse."

He suddenly glared at her and said, "So you checked the medicine cabinet on my side of the sink?"

"Not until I was pretty sure of what I would find," she replied. "At the beginning of the pandemic I attributed your mood swings to being stuck at home, the worries of contracting Covid, and the stress about the finances of Basic Wrappers. As the weeks turned into months, your mood fluctuations worsened and I could see a physical change in you. You turned into a craving beast before each new fix."

He cried out, "I can't believe it's that obvious!"

"To most people it's not. You function okay as far as others can see. I'm pretty sure you are able to hide your addiction from everyone except me and the kids, who know you extremely well."

"The kids know about it?"

Candy replied, "They don't know what causes your mood swings but they're aware that there is something wrong with you. The other day I overheard an exchange between the two. They had finished building a complicated Lego project and Sophia said, 'Let's show Daddy,' to which Mike replied, 'We need to wait until he feels better.'"

Jason was speechless with humiliation.

Candy added, "The only other person who also knows you well is your mom."

"You think she suspects?"

"Maybe. But as you haven't been around her since March, probably not."

"That's a relief."

Jason took a deep breath and then said, "I hate to keep secrets from you, so I'm glad you know. What are you going to do now?"

"Me, nothing," she answered. "You, on the other hand, need to get professional help."

"I will," he promised, "but it'll have to wait until the pandemic is over.

CHAPTER 12

At 8:45 a.m. on Friday, September 18, as Bruce was leaving for his dentist appointment, Cecile was absorbed in an exercise routine. They both had teeth cleaning appointments scheduled six months in advance. She had cancelled hers but Bruce kept his, assuring her that according to the dental office, all precautions would be taken with the hygienist dressed in full preventive gear. That may have been true, but she wasn't up to taking any chances in the dentist chair any time soon.

Cecile was focused on her toned arms workout, casting punches with five-pound dumbbells, when the front doorbell chimed. Who could that be? she wondered. The grocery delivery person was not scheduled to arrive until around ten o'clock. Must be running early, she decided. Hating to interrupt her routine, she nonetheless donned a mask and made her way to the front door and opened it.

"Oh, it's you!" she said.

Without uttering a word, the person at the threshold grabbed her by the throat with gloved hands and squeezed. The ambush had come as a total surprise and to her utter disbelief, making her unable to move at the outset. Then she tried to pry the deadly fingers off her jugular veins, but it was too late. They squeezed even harder and kept the pressure on, even after she became limp. The culprit then let go of her throat and watched as she collapsed, landing in a heap at the bottom of the doorway. The entire act had barely taken more than two minutes. The person nodded, then abruptly turned around and walked away from the scene without another glance in her direction.

***

The young woman who delivered the groceries and the gardener, Raul Ibarra, arrived simultaneously, both parking their vehicles at the curb in front of the Horton residence. Raul was in the process of lifting the lawnmower out of his truck bed when he heard a horrendous scream. He left the mower on the street and rushed toward where the loud shriek had come from. Since the maple tree in the yard blocked his view to the front entrance, he did not come upon the dreadful scene until entering the walkway to the house.

At first glance Raul only saw the young woman, who had dropped both grocery bags, standing in front of the open door, trembling and in shock. A can of tuna fish had escaped from one of the carriers and rolled away, vanishing into a bush which flanked the path, but she didn't seem to notice.

The gardener touched her lightly on the shoulder, asking, "Is everything okay?"

She did not answer, and it wasn't until she took a step to the side that he noticed the figure lying inside the doorway.

"*Madre de Dios*, that's Mrs. Horton!" he cried out.

With a shaky voice the young woman asked, "Is she dead?"

Raul reached for Cecile's limp hand and checked for a pulse. Finding none, he bowed his head and crossed himself, then called 911.

When Bruce came back from the dentist at a quarter past ten, the grocery deliverer's car and the gardener's truck were still parked near the house, and he found the driveway to his garage blocked by police vehicles. There was yellow crime tape barring the front entrance to the house and he got a glimpse of the forensic photographer hard at work.

With a pounding heart he left his car in front of his next-door neighbor's residence, just as the coroner drove up and did likewise.

CHAPTER 13

Lieutenant Claudia Campbell of the Monrovia City Police Detective's Department was put in charge of the homicide investigation. She came from a line of law enforcers. Dad and grandpa had been cops, and at 38, she had one-and-a-half decades as a police officer under her belt. A brief marriage in her early twenties had failed. So far, she had shied away from another attempt at matrimony. She went on occasional dates, nothing serious, but her main focus and purpose in life was her job.

The woman was well liked and respected among her peers in the police force, even though she didn't socialize much. When on duty, her light-brown hair was always restrained in a strict bun and her attractive face wore barely a touch of makeup.

She was getting her routine testing for Covid-19 out of the way and looked forward to a nice lunch break on that Friday when her order was issued and she was briefed. Lunch would have to be eaten on the run, she decided.

On the drive over to the Horton residence, the condition of the world in general, and of Southern California's Monrovia in particular, weighed on her mind. The *Black Lives Matter* movement, although justified, caused a lot of turmoil all over the United States and beyond. There was no disputing that bad police officers did exist, but the majority were honorable people. Defunding the police was not the answer.

Not only had her community to deal with the pandemic and public unrest, but the *Bobcat* fire was still an immediate threat. She applauded the brave firefighters who continued to risk their lives on the front line. She sniffed and thought the air is starting to get better, but the enormous brushfire won't be fully contained for another month.

On the home front, if things continued in the current fashion, her department soon would experience a shortage of staff. She had learned only yesterday that Sprint, her close colleague, had contracted the virus last week. Nobody in the department used his real name. He was the fastest runner they knew, so the nickname *Sprint* stuck. She made a mental note to e-mail him to inquire how he was doing.

The number of people who had fallen victim to Covid-19 and had either died or lay critically ill at hospitals in California, the rest of the States, and all over the world, was staggering. Doctors and nurses were overwhelmed and exhausted, working longer shifts than ever. Hospitals ran short of ventilators and other necessary equipment to keep patients alive. Some needed to turn patients away for lack of beds.

And now we have a homicide, she mused. Fortunately, murders happen seldom in our neck of the woods.

While in line at a fast-food drive-through, Claudia Campbell dwelled on the murder investigation she was assigned to. All she knew from the briefing was that a 69-year-old woman named Cecile Long-Horton had been strangled at her residence. The corpse was found by a grocery delivery person and a gardener, who were both interviewed on the spot and then let go. She had scanned the report of their statements and considered talking to them later but doubted that either one could shed light on the case. She would interview Bruce Horton, the victim's husband, first and then go from there.

Parked in front of the Horton residence, she checked the time. It was 1:20 p.m. Hoping the coroner had some preliminary results for her, she called him.

"I haven't finished the autopsy and can only give you my initial findings" he said. "Neither have I written up a report yet, because I need to do a final analysis first. I take it, you only want the essentials?"

"Essentials are appreciated," she replied.

So he stated, "Manual strangulation by someone who wore surgical gloves was the cause of death. I take it, you don't want the exact medical breakdown?"

"No, only your estimated time of death."

"The approximate time of demise was between 9:00 a.m. and 10:00 a.m." He added, "Closer to nine but not before nine," I would say.

CHAPTER 14

They were seated in the study, six feet apart, facing one another. The victim's and also Bruce Horton's initial data - - like name, date of birth, marital status, profession, et cetera - - had already been established by the 911 responders. So Claudia was glancing at her tablet with that information before starting the interview. Looking up in Bruce's direction, she realized with sudden annoyance that it was hard to determine the man's frame of mind with most of his face covered with his mask. There was pain and sadness in his eyes, she thought, or could it be fear? Granted, hours had passed since his initial shock and he seemed to have his emotions back in control.

She said, "This may be painful for you, but I need to have some basic questions answered about what happened this morning."

He nodded.

"When did you last see your wife alive?"

He did not reply but asked, "Is it Lieutenant Campbell?"

"I do have a lieutenant rank but prefer to be called "Detective."

He nodded again.

At that moment his cell phone rang. He glanced at it but did not answer the call, saying, "Not important. It can wait."

"Now, Mr. Horton, please answer the question."

He said, "Cecile was wrapped up in her exercise routine when I looked in to let her know I was leaving for my dental appointment."

"At what time was that?"

"Quarter to nine." And he murmured, "I wish I'd listened to her."

"What do you mean?" the detective asked.

With a pained expression he explained, "Because of the pandemic, my wife wanted me to cancel the appointment. Had I listened to her, the murderer would not have dared to attack her with me around." He added, "The killer must have waited nearby until he saw me drive away, then - -" Overwhelmed, Bruce did not finish the sentence.

Claudia did not point out that the criminal most likely would have found another opportunity to do the deed. Instead, she asked, "Are you telling me that you saw something or someone suspicious as you went out your front door?"

"No, Detective Campbell, I didn't. I had no cause to be on the lookout for anything suspicious. Besides, I went out the side door, leading to the garage."

"Makes sense." Then she asked, "At what time did you come back from your appointment?"

"I didn't check the time, but I left the dentist's office around ten and it is a ten to fifteen minute drive home, depending on traffic." He was getting annoyed and added, "Check with your people. My driveway was swarming with cops when I came back."

She glanced at her tablet and stated, "It was exactly 10:16 a.m. when you and the coroner arrived simultaneously. I knew this but needed your account."

He inhaled and said, "So you're checking for alibi?"

"Correct. It's basically a formality but you need to give me your dentist's contact information at the end of the interview."

"So you think it was an inside job, as the saying goes. I can understand that, since nothing was stolen or ransacked, but I assure you, there is nobody else living with us."

She was about to ask the next question when he burst out, "If only we had installed a front-door surveillance camera, we'd have a picture of the swine!"

"You planned to install a security system?"

"When I learned of some burglaries in the neighborhood about a year ago, I made the suggestion but Cecile was against it."

"Why?"

"She said that when burglars see a surveillance camera, they figure that there must be tons of valuables in the place."

"Interesting," said the detective.

The landline phone rang. Bruce let the answering machine kick in. The device was in the next room but the caller's voice who left a message was loud enough for them to hear.

He relaxed and said, "Just another telemarketer."

She skimmed her tablet again and asked, "Your wife's occupation is listed as entrepreneur and the company name as Basic Wrappers. What kind of a business is that?"

"They mainly manufacture basic items for restaurant chains, such as aprons, uniforms, table cloths, and so forth. Hair salons and party costume outfits are also among their clientele."

"Are you involved in the business?"

"No," he replied. "Actually, I know little about it. But Cecile's two sons and daughter work there."

"I see. It's a family-owned business. They are all partners?"

"Just employees. My wife is - - I mean was - - the sole owner."

"I was going to ask you about next of kin but you beat me to it. I assume that they are not your sons and daughter?"

"That's right. They're kids from her first marriage. Cecile was a widow when I met her."

"Now let's get back to what happened. Did your wife have any enemies?"

He took a moment to reflect and then replied, "She may have run into some disgruntled competitors in four decades as owner of the company. Cecile was a shrewd businesswoman, but enemies - - no way."

"I meant more in terms of her private life."

Shaking his head, he said, "I can't say that she made enemies."

"Think hard. Was there anyone who had a grudge against her or maybe felt threatened by her?"

He was starting to shake his head again but stopped himself, mumbling, "Oh - - but that's absurd."

Her alert heightened, the detective said, "Tell me what's on your mind."

He hesitated, then disclosed, "Her kids have not been pleased lately, but there is no way they would resort to a physical attack of their mother."

"I'd like to hear what's troubling you, Mr. Horton."

He had no choice but to inform her of what he had overheard of their Zoom board of directors' meeting.

She listened carefully and then said, "So there was a major dispute about whether or not face masks would still be free of charge in the future or, if the business was to survive, they needed to be sold."

"Cecile made it clear that they would always be gratis."

"Do you believe that with less income, her children's livelihoods would have been endangered?"

"I know nothing about their finances."

"What was the 'bad apple' remark all about?"

"I have no idea," he said. "I asked Cecile who and what she meant by the comment, but she kept it a secret."

There was a pause. Then Detective Campbell inquired, "Speaking of your stepchildren, have you let them know what happened?"

He tapped his forehead and cried out, "I totally forgot! I guess I need to call them as soon as you leave."

She reflected for a moment, and then said, "These are unprecedented times and call for unorthodox actions. No need to put anyone at risk by coming to the police station or having them all gather at your residence. I may interview each suspect individually in the future but would appreciate if you'd arrange for a Zoom meeting with your stepchildren later in the day. If so, we can break the bad news to them together."

"No problem," he said, "but I didn't mean to imply that they are *suspects*."

"You didn't, but from my point of view, everyone is."

"What do I tell them the meeting is about?"

"Say that there is urgent news." She handed him her business card and checked the time. "It is almost 2:30.

Please arrange the meeting for four o'clock, then e-mail me the link and confirm the meeting. I'll be at the station."

She got to her feet, saying, "That covers all I need to know for now. As my investigation progresses, I may need your assistance again in the future. Don't bother getting up. I'll let myself out. See you virtually at four," and she left.

Bruce sat for a long time, staring into space. This must be a bad dream, he thought, and I'll wake up at any moment.

CHAPTER 15

Part of the reason Lieutenant Campbell had asked for the Zoom meeting was to witness her suspects' reactions when informed of their mother's homicide. She would have the rare privilege of seeing them without masks.

As for Bruce, he was relieved of not having to be the sole bearer of the sad news to Cecile's offspring. If Detective Campbell was willing to share that responsibility, she was more than welcome.

At four o'clock as the Zoom session took place, the first thing Jason said, "So Bruce, what the hell is this mysterious meeting you called behind Mom's back all about?"

Before Bruce got a chance to answer, Darrell jumped in and pointed at his far-right corner of the screen, demanding, "Who is that person?"

"Detective Campbell of the Monrovia City Police Department," said Bruce.

The siblings' expressions were full of surprise and apprehension as the detective decided to take over, stating, "I'm sorry to inform you of painful news. Your mother was killed this morning."

There was a moment of silence while they all seemed to be stunned by taking in the fact.

The detective observed their faces. There was a remarkable resemblance between the three. They all had either ash blond or light brown hair with light eyes. The men's features were a bit more chiseled than Julie's, but overall they looked alike.

Julie asked, "A traffic accident?"

"No. She was strangled."

Campbell watched their faces with keen attention. Julie let out a shrill shriek, Darrell gasped for air, and Jason tried to control his hands from shaking. The news was no doubt a colossal shock to them, unless one of the three was a good actor. After the initial blow, and as the reality seemed to sink in, they had tons of questions.

The detective did not address any of their queries but said, "I am in charge of the case and so far only at the beginning of the investigation. All I'm at liberty to tell you is that the homicide took place at the entrance of your mother's residence this morning, Friday, September 18, between 9:00 a.m. and 10:00 a.m., according to the coroner."

At the mention of the word "coroner" there was another shrill outcry from Julie and the two brothers just stared.

Before anyone had a chance to inquire further, Detective Campbell stated, "I looked up the Basic Wrappers website and am familiar with your positions within the company but would like to put faces to names. Please introduce yourselves and also give me your contact information. This meeting is a preliminary introduction. I plan to interview each of you in person at a later date."

They had no choice but to comply and did so, one by one.

That settled, she continued, "Meanwhile, I'd like you all to think about your mother's disposition in recent months. Did she make enemies? Was she afraid of anyone? Did you see any change in her? That sort of thing. No need to tell me at this moment; reflect on it and we'll discuss the possibilities during our interviews.

"And now to a more personal matter. I understand that you all had a disagreement with your mother regarding decisions on how to proceed in these financially stressful times of the pandemic. Since she was the sole owner of Basic Wrappers, her position prevailed and she also suggested a 50 percent cut of all your salaries." She looked straight into the camera and asked, "Is this information I have correct?"

There was disbelief and anger in all their faces, but they did not dispute the accuracy of the detective's statement.

"One more thing: What did Cecile Long-Horton mean with her accusation that there was a 'bad apple' among you?"

Now there was obvious fear registered in the faces that stared back at her from each Zoom square.

Darrell recovered first and said, "I have no idea! Ask Bruce, he seems to know everything and doesn't mind blabbing."

"How about you, Mr. *Jason* Long?"

Trying hard to keep his hands from shaking, Jason replied, "I don't know what and who she meant." And he shot an angry glance at Bruce's square and added, "If Mom told you about that remark, it was in strict confidence, and it was spiteful of you to repeat it to the detective."

Julie was beyond words and shook her head.

"That wraps it up," the detective said. "Thank you all for your cooperation. I'll be in touch to schedule interviews. I'll inform you, Mr. Horton, as soon as the coroner releases the body, so that you can make arrangements."

"Arrangements?"

"Concerning the funeral," she said, and signed off.

Everyone else stayed connected and Bruce said, "The detective is right. We'll have to discuss what to do about the funeral, but I can't think straight yet. I'll keep in touch," and he was also gone.

Jason said, "What a nightmare! I can't believe it's true."

"Who could have killed her?" Darrell asked.

Julie cried out, "Oh my God! It just hit me; Mom is really dead," and she broke down sobbing.

At that point, the siblings also disconnected.

***

Campbell stayed seated at her desk and reflected. Did the Zoom meeting she had just left advance her case? Not really. The suspects had all reacted as expected. She was a bit surprised that no tears had been shed at the discovery that their mother had been killed. That may come later though, after the shock wore off. They each looked angry when they learned that she knew about their mother's proposed 50 percent reduction in pay. Whether their wrath was directed at Bruce for letting the cat out of the bag, or at their mother for prompting the pay cut to begin with, was unclear.

She was certain, however, of detecting panic in each of their faces when she mentioned the "bad apple" remark Cecile Long-Horton had made to them - - an indication that each of the three had something to hide. The upcoming individual interviews with these suspects might be interesting, she thought.

She checked the time. Not even five o'clock yet. She decided to drive back to the victim's street and check if any of the Hortons' neighbors had seen anything out of the ordinary.

CHAPTER 16

Detective Campbell listened to the weather forecast on her way to Jason Long's residence in Sierra Madre mid-morning on Monday, September 21. Another hot day lay ahead with temperatures in the 90s. Could be worse, she thought. Last week it was over 100 degrees. She drove past the quaint center town with its village-like feeling and followed the main road upward, until she turned into a side street, only a block away from the Angeles Forest Mountains. Once she arrived at the address in her GPS, she parked on the driveway of the two-story Craftsman-style home. There was barking coming from inside the house as soon as the detective killed the engine.

She was about to ring the doorbell when Candy hurried along the outside of the house, wearing a t-shirt and shorts plus the obligatory mask and introduced herself as Jason's spouse. She cheerfully said, "This way, please," leading them through a gate to the backyard.

Candy chatted on, "Having the interview outside is safer and more convenient. Besides, it keeps Bigfoot, our labrador retriever, from getting too excited and the kids from eavesdropping. They're upstairs in class right now, but one never knows."

They passed by a golf bag with an assortment of clubs leaning against the outside wall of the house, and the detective asked, "You play?"

"I don't. Those are Jason's. He played on Thursday but hasn't gotten around to cleaning his equipment yet."

The covered patio was furnished with a table and chairs, a barbecue grill, and a porch swing. There was a doghouse a short distance away with a water dish and a couple of canine toys in front of it.

Candy motioned the detective into a chair and, pointing to a small container of bottled water sitting on the table, said, "I placed that there for you a moment ago and washed my hands thoroughly first." She continued, "You must want to get down to business. I'll get my husband," and she vanished through the patio sliding glass door.

That's one optimistic woman, Campbell thought, treating me as if I was a friend invited to a garden party.

There was nothing jovial about Jason Long as he stepped outside. He was not exactly hostile, but clearly on edge, which was understandable under the circumstances.

He plopped himself into a garden chair and said, "I hope you catch the killer soon so we can get justice for Mom. I've been pondering what you said in the meeting about her disposition lately and whether she'd made enemies. I cannot come up with anything. It goes without saying that she - - like anyone else on this planet - - felt trapped at home during the current pandemic restrictions, but I believe she tried to make the best of the situation. And as far as making enemies, that wasn't the case. Mom is - - I mean was - - well-liked."

Campbell said, "You work from home these days?"

"Sure do. Ever since March."

"Do you have a special workroom?"

"My desk is in the den. What have all these questions got to do with Mom's attack?"

"As a formality, I need to go over your movements of last Friday, September 18."

"I was home all day," he said, eyeing her with apprehension.

"I'm specifically interested in the morning hours, let's say from around 8:45 a.m. until about 10:00 a.m.?"

He jumped to his feet and yelled, "You've got some nerve, suggesting I drove to Monrovia and killed my mother!"

"Calm down, Mr. Long. I'm not suggesting anything but am required to look into everyone's alibi. So please answer the question."

Jason sat back down and insisted, "I was here all day, like I said. During the time you mentioned, I was in the den, at my desk, working."

"Your wife can confirm that?"

"Definitely."

"Do you get along well with your siblings?"

"What a weird thing to ask. We work together and have to get along."

"And with your stepfather?"

"My what? Oh, Bruce! I never thought of him as stepfather but I guess he is. What about him?"

"Do you two get along?"

"We don't have much in common, but sure, we get along."

A hummingbird flew to the feeder hanging from a beam nearby. They watched the small creature reaching into the hole of the feeder to extract nectar with its long bill. The little bird's wings never stopped flapping like tiny propellers. When satisfied, the little guy flew off in a flash.

Campbell continued with her line of thought and said, "The reason I asked is that during our Zoom session the other day I got the feeling that you resented him."

"Oh, that! I was mad at him and still am. He had no right to tell you about what I consider family business."

"You mean that your mother as CEO of the company suggested that all officers take a 50 percent cut in salary and that you, your brother, and your sister had a heated argument with her about it?"

"Exactly. He was out of line to mention our board meeting's discussion to you. I'm surprised that Mom told him about it to begin with. As a rule she separated Basic Wrappers from her private life."

The detective kept the knowledge that Bruce Horton had in fact overheard the conversation of the board's Zoom meeting to herself and inquired, "Have you given the 'bad apple' comment some more thought?"

"No, and I'm not going to waste my time thinking about it. I have no idea what she meant by the remark."

Jason started to get restless and Campbell noticed that he clutched his hands together in an effort to keep them steady. She wondered what brought on this sudden nervousness and had a strong feeling that he was aching to leave.

At the moment the detective could not think of anything more to discuss. Chances were that he would no longer be cooperative in his present anxious condition anyway, so she decided to end the interview and said, "Thank you for your time, Mr. Long. Please ask your wife to come outside, I'd like to have a word with her too."

CHAPTER 17

It was getting warm and Campbell took off her suit jacket, draping it over the backrest of the patio chair. Thankful for the bottled water Mrs. Long had provided, she drank a couple of sips while she heard the lady of the house order, "Not now, Bigfoot! Stay!"

The sliding glass door opened and Candy appeared, commanding, "Sit!"

As she closed it from the outside, Bigfoot let out one lonely bark and then stationed himself five inches from the glass door on the inside, determined to keep an alert watch.

Candy sat down in the chair vacated by Jason, checked the time, and said, "The kids are still in class but in case they come down, I'd rather they don't know who you are. They do know that their grandmother died but think it was from natural causes. For now, Jason and I would like to keep it that way. In the last few months I kept to social distancing and visited with friends in our yard, so they'd assume that we know each other socially."

"No problem." Then the detective came to the point, mentioning, "Your husband seems to be under tremendous stress."

"Well, yeah! As the CFO of Basic Wrappers he is stressed to the max about the company's survival. On top of that, he has to deal with the death of his mother."

"Are you worried about your own finances since your husband is taking a 50 percent cut in salary?"

"So you know about that? We'll be fine," Candy assured her.

"Can you tell me about the relationship you had with Cecile Long-Horton?"

"That's a strange question. She was my mother-in-law."

"I meant, did you two get along?"

After a pause, Candy said, "I never thought about it but yes, overall we did."

The detective knew there was more to come and waited.

Sure enough, her suspect continued, "I admired Cecile and what she'd accomplished. Bringing up three children on her own while at the same time starting a business from scratch, making it a success, took guts and lots of hard work."

"But?"

"She wasn't the hugging, kissing type of person. Even though she was good to the kids, she didn't shower them with grandmotherly warmth. In other words, she shied away from getting too close to people. The only exception may have been Bruce."

"Oh yes, what do you think of Bruce?"

"In my opinion, he was the best thing that happened to Cecile. Before he appeared on the scene, Basic Wrappers was her whole life. She barely even took vacations. Thanks to Bruce in the last ten years, she learned to enjoy life, going on cruises and socializing with friends a bit."

Campbell got to the crux of the matter and said, "Your husband maintained that he stayed at your residence all day last Friday. Can you attest to that?"

"Absolutely. He's always home now. Other than a trip to the pharmacy to have his prescription refilled and an occasional stroll around the neighborhood, he stays put."

The detective stated, "You said earlier that your husband played golf last Thursday."

"I forgot about that. He did play a short round on Thursday for the first time in months. Golf courses are open and I'm real glad that Jason took it up again. I think it's good for him."

"Getting back to last Friday, I am specifically interested in the time from 8:45 a.m. to 10:00 a.m. Did you see him at his desk in the den or anywhere else in the house during those 75 minutes?"

Candy stammered, "Oh my God! Is that the time Cecile was - - I mean - - died?"

"Approximately, yes. Please answer the question."

"You can't seriously think that Jason had anything to do with it!" Then she reflected and replied, "We took Bigfoot for a walk like we do every morning but - -"

The detective interrupted, "Who do you mean by 'we'?"

"The kids and I."

"So you were gone and came back at what times?"

"I didn't check."

"Approximately?"

Candy blinked a couple of times and then said, "We left before nine, I think, and had to be back by 9:30 for the kids' classes." And she emphasized, "Jason was here the entire time; he was still in his PJ's when we came back."

It was clear that her suspect was shaken up by the turn the conversation had taken. To put her back at ease, Campbell glanced in the direction of the sliding glass door and remarked, "Bigfoot. What an interesting name for a dog!"

"We found him abandoned at our town's Memorial Park and took him home with us. When nobody claimed him after we attached flyers on telephone poles all over the neighborhood and posted his picture on social media, we decided to keep him. He was only a puppy then with enormous paws and the rest of his body hadn't caught up yet. So the kids named him Bigfoot."

Knowing that they were talking about him, the pet wagged his tail, expecting to be let outside. Detective Campbell decided to let both owner and dog off the hook and broke off the interview.

CHAPTER 18

Meanwhile, Julie tried to keep it together all morning at the El Monte plant. She sat at the desk in her office cubicle, fenced in by transparent plastic shields, staring at paperwork she was unable to focus on. There was some comfort in the familiar rhythmic rattling of her employees' sewing machines, but there was nothing comforting nor familiar in the thoughts that she could not ban from her mind.

Mom was dead! The reality of it had only begun to sink in. Overall, Mom had done a good job raising her and her brothers. On an adult level, however, the two women had had nothing in common other than Basic Wrappers. And the thought hit her: she will no longer be calling the shots at Basic Wrappers. The very fact scared and thrilled her at the same time. Who was going to take over as CEO? she wondered. Probably Jason. Although Darrell was cocky enough to try to convince them he might be a better choice for the position. No matter who was going to become the new chief executive, either brother would have a hard time filling Mom's shoes. We may have not seen eye to eye with her lately, but there is no dispute that she knew how to lead a company. In fact, she was darn good at it.

Then she reflected on a more pressing concern. Like the detective had said, they'd have to make funeral arrangements. She hadn't discussed it with Mateo yet but felt strongly about not having Michelle attend. Flying was dangerous at present and she didn't want their daughter to take the risk. In the current virus situation she imagined that only a few people, like the immediate family, were permitted to attend. Considering Mom's violent death, this was in fact a blessing in disguise. Best leave the funeral details up to Bruce, she determined.

She hadn't had the courage to inform her workers of the tragedy yet. They needed to be told before Detective Campbell arrived for the interview. She thought, oh my God, what is the officer going to grill me about? And how can I prepare for the answers if I don't know the questions? Julie decided to worry about it later. Right now, she'd have lunch and then she'd slip up to the conference room one last time.

As two of the seamstresses watched their boss disappear on the stairs to the second floor, the first one said, "I wonder what Señora Martinez is doing up there every day?"

"Whatever it is, she comes back down energized," remarked the second.

"Could be she's listening to music and dances, or does yoga. Or maybe she's playing interactive action video games!"

"For all we know she goes up to pray."

"Taking her purse along?"

"What she's doing is none of our business," the other said, and that ended their conversation.

Julie locked the door to the second story behind her and climbed the stairs, thinking, just one more time and then I'll quit.

Seated at the head of the long conference room table, she reached into her purse and - - "Oh no!" she couldn't help shrieking, as she realized that her special phone was missing. She searched every compartment of the purse, then took all items out, one by one, and laid them on the table. Her regular phone was there but not the crucial one. With a pounding heart she turned the empty bag upside down and shook it. There was nothing left in there but the lining.

In a panic, she thought back to her movements at home of that morning and remembered having changed purses. She must have left her secret phone on the dresser. "Julie, you screwed up big time!" she told herself. Would Mateo question what the strange phone was doing in their house, she wondered. Her husband was a trusting soul, but he may be curious and dial some contact numbers. Her only hope was to beat him home before he could discover the phone's existence. Rats, she couldn't leave work early because she had to sit through an interview with the detective, scheduled for late afternoon.

CHAPTER 19

As luck had it, Julie and Mateo arrived home simultaneously. All is not lost, Julie thought, and raced past him, saying, "I'm in a hurry to use the bathroom."

To her dismay, the phone was not on the dresser when she got to the master bedroom. In a frenzy, she ran over to the closet and reached for her other purse, which turned out to be empty.

She let out a faint cry as she looked up and saw Mateo standing at the open door.

"Are you looking for this, *Brigitte?*" he asked, holding up her special phone.

Julie paled and for the moment could not speak.

Mateo thundered, "What the devil is going on? I came home for lunch and heard this phone ring. When I answered it, a guy asked for Brigitte. I told him he had the wrong number. Five minutes later, another person called, demanding to speak with Brigitte. And then yet another was on the line with the same request. What's with this phone and what the hell are you up to?"

Julie recovered and said, "I can explain."

"You'd better!"

"Can we discuss it over dinner? All I have to do is warm up yesterday's leftovers."

"No! I want to hear it right here and now," he shot back.

Julie sat down on the edge of their king-size bed, fighting back tears of guilt. Mateo stayed standing, his intense stare firm.

Having him tower over her in that fashion was intimidating, but she gave herself a mental push and started her confession by saying, "Remember my friend Suzanne?"

"Vaguely."

"Anyhow, she called me at the beginning of the lockdown to see how I was doing. We had a nice chat and as I was about to end the call, she remarked, 'You have a sexy voice.' Naturally, I was flattered."

"Flattered that a woman called you sexy?"

"Not sexy," she corrected, "only a sexy voice. Suzanne went on, telling me that they could use me in her line of business."

Mateo roared, "And what the hell kind of business is that?"

"I'm getting to it," Julie replied. And, moving a tad away from him, she continued, "Suzanne explained it all to me. What it amounts to is phone sex. Apparently, Suzanne had done it in her spare time for months. She talked me into joining, saying that I would be doing lonely and desperate men a favor, especially during these restrictive times of the pandemic. She explained that I would be anonymous and would choose a persona name, and that I could sign up for as much or little time as I wanted to. I'd be given a phone that would be used for phone sex only."

She sighed and concluded, "So I agreed to give it a try. You already know that I chose the fantasy name of Brigitte. I committed to three-quarters of an hour during my lunch break, Monday through Friday. I had an average of three clients a day, about 15 minutes each. Some called one time only, others were regulars."

She gave him a pleading look and stated, "I was going to quit today, I swear."

"What's wrong with our sex that you had to resort to this phone sex thing?" Mateo yelled.

"Absolutely nothing! I'm satisfied with what we have. You know that."

"Then why?"

"You've got this all wrong. There was nothing sexual in it for me. I was basically doing the guys a favor."

"By talking dirty?"

"Not always. Some just needed an emotional outlet. A person who listens to their problems."

"I don't care what they needed. And I can picture what kind of perverted problems they wanted to discuss. Did you get paid for your services?"

"Very little for less than an hour a day, as you can imagine. I didn't do it for the money, that's for sure."

He pointed an accusing finger at her and said, "For the thrill of being in charge, then! You are basically a phone whore."

Those words hit her worse than a slap in the face. She stayed sitting on the bed long after he had stormed off. From one day to the next, life had come crashing down on her. She not only had to deal with her mom's murder, but her husband's mistrust and wrath.

CHAPTER 20

On that Monday night, Darrell and Sybille lay awake after turning off the lights. Sybille was about to start a critical conversation when her husband reached for her.

"Seriously?" she exclaimed. "How can you think of sex in our situation?"

"It relaxes me," he replied.

"Forget the relaxing and let's talk." She took a deep breath and stated, "We need to get our stories straight."

"What do you mean?"

"Don't act dumb. The female detective is going to interview us tomorrow."

"So?"

"She's going to look into alibis."

"I have nothing to worry about," he said. "According to the detective, Mom was killed Friday morning. As you know, I was driving home from Vegas on Friday. There is a hotel record to show I was there overnight."

"When did you leave town and at what time did you get home?"

"Early, I wanted to be here before eleven. But you know that; you saw me when I got back. What's all this interrogation?"

"Don't you see? You can't prove where you were at the time of the murder."

Darrell sat up in bed and said, "We don't know the exact time; all the detective said that it happened between nine and ten."

"Exactly! You could have stopped in Monrovia on your way back."

"Are you insane? I didn't kill Mom!"

"I'm not saying that you did, but you could have, as far as that cop is concerned."

"So what do you suggest?"

Sybille let out a nasty laugh and said, "Since you're so keen on betting, our best bet is to say that we can vouch that both of us were home all morning last Friday."

While he was thinking this over, Sybille continued, "We have to be prepared that the authorities will look into our finances and our standard of living. Among other things, your major gambling problem will come to light and the fact that we can't survive a 50 percent reduction of your salary."

He said, "I planned to call Mom and plead with her to have a change of heart about the pay cut, but never got around to it."

"That's a good strategy; run with that."

"What the heck do you mean?"

"Tell the detective that you called your mother, begging her to change her mind, and that she was willing to think about it."

Then Sybille sat up too and, trying to make out his body language in the dark, asked, "So how did the poker game go?"

He sighed and replied, "I won big time at first, then lost it all in the end. I promise, I'll go for help soon!"

"You do that, or I can't guarantee to stand by you any longer."

After a prolonged pause Darrell said, "Mom may have been misguided about the masks and also about tightening our belts, like she put it, but she was a good mother and had our best interests at heart."

Sybille, who had never seen eye to eye with her mother-in-law, realized that he needed to mourn her at that moment and reached over to squeeze his hand.

CHAPTER 21

On Thursday, September 24, Detective Campbell called Sprint, her colleague. A few days before, the two had corresponded via e-mail. At that time he had been feeling miserable, due to being ill with Covid-19.

He picked up on the second ring and Campbell asked, "How're you feeling?"

"Much better," he replied, "but I'm under quarantine and bored. How are things at the department? I expect you're holding the fort."

"That's what I want to talk with you about. I'm assigned to Cecile Long-Horton's murder investigation and could use a sounding board."

Sprint said, "I heard about it on the news. Strangulations don't happen every day in Monrovia, so it couldn't be kept away from the media. About that sounding board; go ahead, I'm listening."

She ran the basics by him, including the coroner's findings, and then said, "Let me tell you what I've done so far. I checked out the neighbors on each side of the victim's house, plus the one across the street. Nobody saw anything, which isn't surprising. There is no direct view from the next-door houses to the front door of the Horton residence, and a large maple tree blocks its sight from the house across the street."

She continued, "I've interviewed every suspect I can think of but am not much further in my investigation than when I started, and - - -"

"Think it's an inside job?"

Campbell stated, "It wasn't a burglary gone wrong; the perpetrator never stepped inside the house. And I don't believe for a moment the strangler was either a serial killer or a demented person, ringing people's doorbell and then going for anyone's throat who shows up. No, this was done by someone the victim knew, most likely by one of her family members." And she related the argument overheard by Bruce Horton that Cecile had had during an online board meeting with her sons and daughter.

"As I said, I've interviewed all concerned, unless I missed somebody or something. You know how I proceed by taking notes, either during or right after an interview. The only two suspects who have a proven alibi are Bruce Horton, the victim's husband, and Mateo Martinez, her daughter's spouse. According to the dentist's office, Bruce was sitting in the hygienist's chair at 9:00 a.m. on the morning of the murder and Mateo had two co-workers attest that he was on the job during the entire time that the killing could have taken place. Everyone else's alibi is doubtful at best.

"I checked out driving times personally, so I'll run everyone's claims by you. Jason and Candy Long live in Sierra Madre; it takes 10 minutes to get from their house to the victim's. Jason said he was home all day on Friday, September 18. His wife verified the fact but was gone herself to walk their dog around the time of the murder. Darrell and Sybille Long live in San Marino, an 11- minute ride from Monrovia. They both vouch for having been home together all morning of said Friday."

She continued, "Julie Martinez claimed to have overslept on that particular day. She stated she left her house at 9:15 a.m. and arrived at work before 9:30, instead of nine o'clock. She has her employees as witnesses that she did in fact arrive at work shortly before 9:30, but she has nobody to confirm that she left her house at 9:15, since her husband had long left for his job by then.

"It takes nine minutes to drive from Duarte to Monrovia and 14 minutes to get from Monrovia to El Monte, where the plant of the family business is located. If Julie left her house at 9 o'clock, just 15 minutes before her claim, she could have easily driven to her mother's house, done the strangulation - - which couldn't have taken more than five minutes - - and then driven herself to the plant in El Monte."

Sprint asked, "What about motive?"

"All siblings had one. Their mother was about to cut their salaries in half. There is also the strange accusation the victim made of one of them being a 'bad apple.'"

"Any clue what that is about?"

"None. I've asked them and they all allege being in the dark of what or who their mother meant by that remark. One of them is lying, that's obvious."

Then she said, "I have all my notes in front of me and can't shake the feeling that I'm missing something important. In your opinion, what should be my next move?"

He asked, "The victim is rich?"

"I believe so."

"Find out what's in her will. Estate lawyers are hard to get information from, but since this is a murder case, the attorney-client privilege may not apply."

"That'll be next on my agenda," she said.

"What impression did you take away from your interviews? Did they show shock and grief when they learned of their mother's murder? And, more importantly, did they overreact with these emotions?"

"Initially, during the group Zoom meeting we first had, they all seemed shocked and in disbelief. Nobody burst out crying, but I think that was because reality hadn't sunk in yet. I know what you mean by 'overreacting.' The culprit would make sure to show that he or she was stunned and overwhelmed by grief. I didn't see any of that. By the time I interviewed each person separately, they were in control of their emotions. I do believe, though, that each had something to hide. The exception was Candy Long, who was open with me and unrestrained. She is one of those happy-go-lucky persons with a confident outlook on life."

Sprint asked, "What vibes did you get about the character of each suspect?"

"Some were hard to read and others like an open book. I'll get to the simple ones to figure out first. Like I already mentioned, Candy is easygoing and uncomplicated. The victim's other daughter-in-law, Sybille, is the total opposite, but also not hard to figure out. I found her domineering, arrogant, and due to her above-average good looks, full of herself. I tag Cecile's son-in-law, Mateo, as a down-to-earth, hardworking man.

"As for the rest of the suspects, husband, sons, and daughter, they are harder for me to make out. Although I'm positive that each one is suffering and mourning his or her loss, I can't shake the feeling that these suspects have something to hide. It may have nothing to do with the murder, though. For instance, Bruce seemed uneasy when the phone rang during our interview on the day of the homicide and relieved when it was just a telemarketer. This may have only been my imagination; it is hard to read expressions when the person is masked. Also, he had learned only hours before of his wife's murder, so his nervousness is understandable.

"There is definitely something wrong with Jason. The man acts normal and then suddenly gets jumpy, like a spooked colt. His brother Darrell is cocky, but I suspect that's an act. He may be insecure under all the bravado. His wife seems to be the driving force in their relationship. Julie, the victim's daughter, is the hardest to read. She comes off as a competent, caring manager, and from what I gathered when interviewing her at the Basic Wrappers plant, is well-liked among her employees. Still, I couldn't shake the idea that there is more to that woman than meets the eye."

"How so?"

"For one thing, she checked the time on her wristwatch twice during our interview, assuming she was unobserved while I was taking notes. Granted, it was close to the end of her working day, but I had the feeling that she couldn't wait to get away from me. It may have had nothing to do with the case or my questioning, but she seemed to be thinking, *Let me go. I need to get home!*"

Then Sprint inquired, "Did you get an idea of what kind of a woman the victim was?"

"Other than she was the CEO and sole owner of Basic Wrappers, a garment manufacturing company, I know nothing about her. So far, no one has volunteered information about her character. I take that back. Candy, her daughter-in-law, did mention that Cecile was not the hugging and kissing type."

"If I were you, I'd try to learn more about the victim."

Campbell said, "Thanks for the tip. It is always good to get someone else's perspective. I won't take up more of your time."

"What time? I have 12 more days of quarantine and am bored out of my skull. Call me day or night for advice or if you just want to think aloud."

With that, they clicked off.

CHAPTER 22

On the following day, Carole Pedrotti was about to run an errand before starting on her late shift from 3:00 to 11:00 p.m. at her grocery store in Pasadena. On the spur-of-the-moment, she changed directions and drove to Bruce's residence instead.

Her mind was racing with anger and frustration. An entire week had passed since Cecile had gotten herself killed, and Bruce was playing hard to get. When she called after the news was out, he insisted that it was for the best if they cool it for a while. Cool it! They'd been cooling it since the beginning of the pandemic. She was not used to being ignored and was not about to put up with it.

By a stroke of luck the man was free now but had no intention of enjoying his freedom. Sure, to the outside world he needed to play the grieving husband, but there was no reason that they couldn't get together. If he was worried about his neighbors, they could rendezvous at her place. Was he really scared of catching Covid? Although the idea felt ridiculous, she would even wear a mask if that made him happy.

All of a sudden she was not so sure of herself and her power over him. What if he actually did mourn his wife? And even worse, what if he had chosen his wife over her in the end? Absurd! Yet, thinking back to their meeting in the park the other day, she had to admit to herself that his attitude toward her may have changed. Well, only one way to find out.

At that point, she had arrived at her destination and noticed a strange car parked in Bruce's driveway.

***

In the study of the Horton residence, Detective Campbell and Bruce were engaged in a conversation. The detective had dropped by to inquire about two topics on her agenda.

First she asked, "You've been informed that your spouse's body has been released. Correct?"

"Yes, two days ago," he replied. "But because of Covid-19, mortuaries are overwhelmed. We can't have a burial until October 1. Until then she's being kept on ice." An involuntary moan escaped him as he said those last words.

"I'm sorry about that, but it will give you adequate time to make arrangements."

Then the detective said, "You realize that I need to look into your wife's will and testament. I presume that she made a will?"

Bruce replied, "She never talked about it, but I'm sure she did. Cecile was precise about legal matters."

"Please give me her estate lawyer's name and contact information."

"I don't know it. Her son Jason would most likely be the one who does," he stated.

Campbell stared at him, openmouthed. And before she could respond to that surprising bit of information, the doorbell rang.

"Excuse me," Bruce said and went to answer it.

When he saw Carole standing there at the doorstep, he wanted to shout, "Turn around and drive away!" but controlled the impulse. The study of the house was right off the front entrance and the detective could easily listen to their conversation.

Instead he said, "Hello there, what brings you here?" while at the same time shaking his head vigorously.

Carole took the hint and said, "I noticed the car in the driveway. If you have company, I'll come back later."

Before she could leave, Campbell appeared and said, "I'm not company, but I am in charge of Cecile Long-Horton's murder investigation. Let me introduce myself. I'm Claudia Campbell of the Monrovia City Police Department. And what is your name?"

The former had no choice but to state it, and the detective continued, "Ms. Pedrotti, if you don't mind waiting a minute or two, Mr. Horton and I are almost done."

Carole said, "That's okay, I'm on my way to work and came by to express my condolences." She touched Bruce's shoulder for a split second and said, "I'm so sorry for your loss. Let me know if there is anything I can do to help." Then she nodded at Detective Campbell, turned on her heels, and briskly walked to where her car was parked.

Bruce and the detective went back to the study and Campbell said, "Now, where were we? Oh, yes. About the will. You mentioned that Jason Long would have the information concerning your wife's estate lawyer. Did she by chance tell you roughly how her money would be disbursed?"

"She didn't, and I never asked."

"Interesting."

"I do know that the deed to this house is registered under both our names. Cecile legally added mine a few years ago."

Detective Campbell said, "That's all the questions I had today. Thank you for your assistance."

She had already taken a couple of steps toward the exit of the room but turned back and said, "One more thing. What is your relationship to Carole Pedrotti?"

Thankful that half of his face was covered, he replied, "We went to high school together."

"And kept in touch all this time?"

Masked or not, this woman would see right through him. It was in his best interest to tell the truth. So he said, "We both went to our class reunion last year and then connected again."

"I see. Did you and Carole Pedrotti see each other during the last month?"

He didn't answer, and she stated, "You'd better tell me. I can get a court order to have your phone records checked."

He broke down and admitted, "We met in the park, just once. And yes, before the pandemic started, we had an affair." And there was hurt and a pleading look in his eyes as he added, "I was going to end the relationship, I swear."

As Detective Campbell drove back to her station, she thought, I've learned more than anticipated from the talk with Bruce Horton. By pure luck I was at his residence at the right time in order to learn of a girlfriend and meet her. And I discovered a victim's trait. Cecile Long-Horton must have been an extremely secretive woman by not disclosing the estate lawyer's information to her husband.

CHAPTER 23

The phone conversation with Jason started off on the wrong foot.

When Detective Campbell requested he provide her with his mother's estate lawyer information, he said, "That is none of your business."

"Under the circumstances, it is."

She had to hold the phone away from her ear as he roared, "If your guess is that Mom was killed because of an inheritance, you've tagged us wrong!"

"Let me make something clear, Mr. Long. I don't make guesses but go by facts. If what you claim is true, you have nothing to worry about by giving me the information."

Reluctantly, he complied and said, "Mom dealt with Eduard Blyte, who is a partner at the Law Offices of Stolzerman, Blyte & Morales. They're in Pasadena, but I don't have their contact information handy."

"Thank you. I'll find them," she said. "Are you familiar with the beneficiaries of your mother's will?"

He stated, "Some 20 years ago, she had a living trust and will drawn. At around the same time, Julie joined the business. Darrell and I were already on board. Mom called a meeting and told us what to expect."

He paused, undecided whether or not to enlighten the detective further. He made up his mind and continued, "I remember Mom saying, 'Just so you are clear, I will never make any of you partners; it is best if I stay the sole owner of the company. You'll have to wait until I retire or die to own the business.'"

He cleared his throat and went on, "Then she told us about the content of the will. Ownership of Basic Wrappers was to be in the names of all three of us after her death. Her private estate was dealt with separately in the will. Except for a couple of legacies to charities, which were listed in the exact dollar amounts, her private assets were also to be equally divided between Darrell, Julie, and me."

He went on, "That was then. Mom never talked about it again. I'm surprised that Bruce couldn't give you the estate lawyer information. I assume she either made a new will or added Bruce to the existing one after they got married."

"I'll find out when I talk with Eduard Blyte. Thanks for the info and for being up front with me, Mr. Long. I do appreciate it," she said, and ended the call.

CHAPTER 24

Detective Campbell had an appointment to see Eduard Blyte on Monday morning, September 28. She took the elevator up to the third floor of the office building on Green Street, in the heart of Old Town Pasadena, and arrived punctually at the offices of Stolzerman, Blyte & Morales.

The door to the law offices waiting room was wide open and she entered the large space. There was no employee behind the impressive reception desk. In fact, there was no one in the entire room. She heard a faint phone conversation going on in one of the interior offices. The only other sound came from a large fan, placed at the entrance.

The detective took a seat in one of the black leather chairs, spaced more than six feet apart, and observed her elegant surroundings. Glass-top end tables flanked the reception chairs. On one of them stood a box of tissues; on the other, what looked to be a live Boston fern. On the wall immediately behind the reception area hung a wrought iron wall clock. Other than two large water colors, spaced far apart, the cream colored walls were left bare. At center stage, there was an aquarium filled with exotic fish, and at the far end of the room she noticed a corner display case. The fluorescent linear ceiling lighting gave the place an airy, clean look.

She thought, whoever designed this outer space not only wanted to make a statement but had genuinely good taste. She got up from the chair and was about to have a closer look at what was exhibited in the display case, when the same male voice she had heard on the phone called out, "I take it that's you out there, Detective Campbell. Stay put, I'm coming."

A second later, a man in his sixties appeared. He had a full mop of white hair and inquisitive gray eyes that peered at her from behind designer glasses. He was in the process of adjusting his face mask with one hand while carrying a file in the other.

He didn't waste time with introductions since they both knew who they were dealing with. "Sorry we can't shake hands," he said, and motioned her back to a chair while pulling another for himself and placing it at an angle where they could face one another.

Then he said, "As you can see, I'm taking every precaution possible. This room is larger than my office, and the fan, which blows in fresh air, should make our meeting safe. My secretary and my partners are working from home these days, unless it is essential that they talk with clients in person. I try to do as much work as I can at home too."

"Thank you for seeing me, Mr. Blyte."

"I do want the murder of Cecile Long-Horton solved and the culprit caught. As I never give out information concerning a client by phone or e-mail, getting together in person is the only way." And his keen eyes searched hers, asking, "Do you have a lead?"

"Not yet. I'm still in the early stages of the investigation. I'm sure you understand that it is crucial that I learn who benefits financially from the victim's death. I talked with her son Jason Long, who told me that your firm drew a will for her 20 years ago. He gave me a rough idea about the beneficiaries of the will. I can imagine that she made changes to it about a decade ago when she married Bruce Horton."

The attorney said, "I haven't even officially contacted the beneficiaries to date. Naturally, I read about the tragedy in the paper. The other day, I called Jason Long to express my condolences, but I wanted to wait until after the funeral - - which he told me wasn't until October 1 - - before I would inform all the heirs concerning the content of the will."

"I understand," she said. "Just acknowledge that Cecile Long-Horton changed or made an addition to her will about ten years ago."

"She did not. At least not at that time."

"Later, then?"

"Much later," Blyte replied. "Mrs. Long-Horton came to see me earlier this year, right before the lockdown." He opened up the file on his lap, found the appropriate information, and stated, "On March 12, 2020, she requested to make an addition to her will."

Puzzled, Campbell asked, "She waited that long before adding her husband?"

"No, she did not add him to her will. Her request was of an entirely different nature."

Tell me already! Campbell thought.

Blyte reached for a silk hanky in his pocket, then wiped his glasses that had fogged up above the mask.

At last he continued, "Mrs. Long-Horton's request was to include a legacy to the will of a substantial amount in favor of - -" he consulted his file again - - "Antonia Silva, her housekeeper."

She stared at him, then inquired, "So Bruce Horton is not mentioned in the will at all?"

He shook his head.

Claudia Campbell later wondered how she made it out of the law offices without stumbling over her own two feet. That last revelation had taken her by total surprise.

CHAPTER 25

The detective decided to follow Sprint's suggestion to try to learn more about the victim's character. She called Candy Long with the request to have another chat. When she asked "How can we do it discreetly," Candy seemed to understand and suggested the detective join her and Bigfoot on their morning walk. She indicated that Wednesday would be a good choice, since her kids had early classes that day and wouldn't accompany them.

This suited Detective Campbell well, giving her time to investigate another case that had been thrown into her lap. She had been tested for Covid-19 on a regular basis and had received her latest result, which was again negative. Others of the Monrovia Police Department were not that lucky; two more officers had tested positive. Consequently, Campbell had been assigned to take over a robbery investigation, as well as following up on a domestic violence case. Both required her mental concentration and a lot of paper work.

By Wednesday morning, she switched to murder mode, once again. The temperature was a pleasant 77 degrees, although the forecast was in the 80s for later in the day. In Sierra Madre, she parked near one of the churches on Baldwin Avenue where they had agreed to meet. Perfect timing, she thought, when spotting Candy and Bigfoot, coming from a side street and walking toward her. Bigfoot wagged his tail in greeting as they reached the detective.

They trekked uphill and Candy said, "I hope you don't mind if we let Bigfoot lead the way. He is set on his routine course."

"Not at all," Campbell replied, watching him with amusement as he pulled at the leash, rushing them upward at a fast pace. After turning right into Mira Monte Avenue, once the two women's breathing had slowed to normal, they started conversing.

The detective said, "The reason I asked for us to meet again is because I'd like to learn more about what kind of person Cecile Long-Horton was. Since you were not blood related, I trust that your account will be neutral."

Candy was in no hurry to answer and took a long time to think it over. When she finally did speak, she said, "If you'd have asked me six or seven months ago, I'd have said that my mother-in-law was an astute businesswoman whose main interest in life was the success of Basic Wrappers. She did love her sons and daughter, but my take was always that those strings were mainly attached to their connection to her business.

"As far as her private life, she did appreciate Bruce for what he'd brought out in her, like going on trips and enjoying the niceties of living a bit. Where her grandkids were concerned - - our two kids and Julie's daughter, who is in college at the moment - - she was generous towards them but as I told you before, not the hugging and kissing type."

Detective Campbell asked, "And now? Was she different lately?"

"Yes. There was a change in her. Not that I observed it firsthand. I only saw her once since the pandemic started, but what I learned from my husband made me come to that conclusion. She became less business oriented and more compassionate toward people. I attributed it to her being scared of contracting Covid-19, but now I'm not so sure."

Bigfoot came to a halt and sniffed around in someone's front yard hedge, undecided whether or not to do his business. Candy was prepared and pulled a plastic baggy out of her shorts' pocket. It was a false alarm. Apparently, the spot was not quite right for him and he moved them along.

"You were telling me about a change in Cecile. Can you give me an example?"

"It concerned the darned cloth masks they sewed at her plant. Not only did Cecile insist that they be produced in huge quantities and shipped free of charge to whoever wanted them, but she personally took boxes filled with masks to skid row and distributed them among the homeless."

"That was indeed a selfless act of kindness and not without risk to herself," Campbell remarked.

"Jason was outraged about it. He didn't think that giving away stuff for free at a time when orders from clients trickled to practically nothing was a good idea to begin with. And the fact that his mom put herself in danger by going to skid row, he considered reckless."

They were walking by the Mount Wilson Trail Park and the detective asked, "Have you ever ventured up that trail?"

"Jason and I did, years ago. It's a bit challenging in some areas but we made the nine-mile hike all the way up to the observatory." She added with a giggle, "That was before we had kids."

They looped to the left and then walked along a street that would take them back to Baldwin Avenue. Bigfoot decided that now was the time to discharge his 'number two' and chose a spot right next to a fire hydrant.

Candy scooped it up expertly into her baggy and said, "These are the chores necessary when owning a dog, but I don't mind. Bigfoot is my big baby."

They were almost back to where the detective's car was parked when she asked, "And what did *you* think of your mother-in-law's action?"

"Although totally out of character, I thought it was wonderful!"

"You mentioned that initially you attributed the change in her to the pandemic, but now you are no longer sure that was the case. What do you have in mind?"

Candy replied, "I can't help feeling that she somehow had a premonition that her life may end soon."

CHAPTER 26

The funeral service was held outdoors at the Forest Lawn Cemetery in Arcadia. The weather was mild on that late morning of October 1. The mourners wore masks and sat in folding chairs, placed six feet apart. This was the first time the family members had gathered in person since March. Even though hugging was impossible under the current circumstances, it should have been natural for them to show some warmth and support. Yet, they looked at each other with suspicion. In addition to the immediate family of the departed, only her housekeeper and gardener were among the bereaved. The grandchildren remained absent, as their parents saw no reason to put them through the experience.

The service was kept short, with a pastor leading them in prayer and then adding a few words of encouragement. He applauded Cecile's accomplishments, praising her dedication to Basic Wrappers, but his speech did not come close to a heartfelt eulogy. The man read from the notes that had been handed to him.

The cremation had taken place earlier, and after the service there was a short ceremony of interring the ashes. There were tears shed as the mourners realized the finality of Cecile's fate. The entire event had not taken more than 20 minutes, which was understandable, given the world health situation of the moment.

Since going to a restaurant for a further gathering was out of the question, Bruce invited everyone to his back patio and pool area for lunch, which he had delivered. Again, it was done with proper social distancing. There were croissant sandwiches with a choice of either turkey/ avocado or ham and cheese, and a variety of beverages. Although cordial on the surface, the group couldn't help being suspicious of one another. Everyone was tongue-tied at first and ate in silence while all sorts of pondering entered their minds.

Bruce thought, the last two weeks have been like a bad dream and I'm afraid the nightmare isn't over yet. Will it ever end?

Julie mused, everyone is aware that one of us is a killer and shivered, even though it was 78 degrees. And then she remembered how angry she herself had been with Mom not long ago. The scene with Mateo came to mind when she'd told him about hating Mom. Oh, she wished she could take it back!

Mateo contemplated, this is an extremely uncomfortable situation. Instead of supporting each other in their grief, this family is full of mistrust.

Darrell thought, I can't stand the tension among us. Why does everyone think we are capable of murder? It could have just as well been an outsider. That woman detective seems to be convinced that the culprit is one of the family. I doubt she's even considering any other possibility. In my opinion, she's incompetent.

Sybille, his wife, was amused and thought, they're distrusting and suspecting each other. What a waste of time and energy. No matter what, they should all be thankful for the outcome. Cecile is no longer calling the shots at Basic Wrappers. Don't they understand that they all can breathe freely now?

Jason endured a powerful headache. It felt like someone was hammering relentlessly at his skull. He thought, I hope we can leave as soon as we're done eating. I need to get home.

Candy thought, I'm so glad we got a sitter for the kids. This would be torture for them. They would sense the bad vibes and know that their relatives are under enormous amounts of pressure, without understanding why. It is hard enough for the adults to cope with the feeling.

Antonia Silva watched the sun reflecting on the surface of the pool while shedding another tear and thought, poor Mrs. Horton, I'm keeping your secret but wonder if you'd want me to reveal it now that you're gone.

The gardener, Raul Ibarra, was trying to come to terms with something on his mind as well. He thought back to the day of the tragedy. After he and the young woman who delivered groceries had discovered Mrs. Horton's body, he'd been in shock and forgotten what he'd witnessed earlier that day. It so happened that he'd driven to the Horton residence twice.

As soon as he'd parked his truck the first time, he realized that he'd left the power cutter in his shed at home. Mrs. Horton had asked him specifically to trim the hedge on the side of the house. So he had turned around and driven back to get it. Only in the last few days did he suddenly remember what he saw on the first occasion. There had to be a harmless explanation, he thought. Should he approach the person now? He'd think about it some more while enjoying the delicious lunch.

Raul was the only person at the gathering who did not feel the tension beneath the forced cordiality among everyone. As soon as he had swallowed the last bite of his sandwich, he happily chatted about looking for a buyer of his bronze collection, and described some of his treasures in detail.

CHAPTER 27

Since Antonia Silva had her elderly mother, husband, and two teenage kids living under the same roof with her, she suggested a meeting in the park for the interview with Detective Campbell. Antonia had a housecleaning job on Friday morning, but was free in the afternoon.

On the drive to Grant Park in Pasadena, a small park not far from where the Silvas lived, the detective smiled to herself. Interviewing suspects had a way of being unconventional, these days. First in the course of walking a dog, and now at a public neighborhood park.

The housekeeper was there first, seated in the shaded picnic area wearing a red top, like she had mentioned when they made the appointment over the phone. There would have been no need to make herself recognizable, since she was the only person at their indicated meeting spot. Campbell introduced herself and sat down on the bench opposite from hers. As they faced one another across the picnic table, keeping the appropriate distance, it was clear to the detective that the woman was extremely nervous.

Before she could put her at ease, Antonia burst out, "I know nothing about Mrs. Horton's murder."

"I'm sure you don't," the detective agreed. "I'd only like to discuss what your job as her housekeeper entailed.

For instance, how often were you at her house and what were your duties?"

Somewhat relieved, the former replied, "I cleaned Mr. and Mrs. Horton's house every Monday, except for during the lockdown. My job was to vacuum and dust the upstairs and downstairs, plus clean the kitchen and bathrooms they used - - the guest bathroom rarely needed cleaning. Every so often, I was asked to do extra work, like washing down the pool deck furniture, or cleaning the ceiling light fixtures, stuff like that."

Antonia continued, "I did not do windows; they had a special crew for that. Mrs. Horton did their own laundry and cooking. She also took care of her indoor plants herself. I helped out with the cooking when they had guests, though. She always paid me extra for additional work."

"You've been their housekeeper a long time?"

"Over ten years." And she choked up when adding, "Mrs. Horton was my best and longest-lasting client."

"You liked working for her a lot, then?"

"Oh yeah, the job was easy enough and with perks too."

"Perks?"

Antonia elaborated, "Mrs. Horton was frugal as a rule, but she loved clothes and had stunning outfits, mostly designer. She was taller than me, but we both wear a size six. She generously handed me down the clothes she no longer wanted." With a twinkle in her eye she added, "I am the best dressed woman among all my relatives and friends!"

Now that the housekeeper had warmed up to her, Campbell said, "You have a good command of the English language, but I do detect an accent. Where are you from?"

"Brazil was my homeland."

"I presume you've lived in the US for a long time?"

"You bet. Our teenage kids were born here."

The detective felt it was time to get down to business and asked, "Do you remember where you were on Friday, September 18, from about 8:45 a.m. until 10:00 a.m.?"

Antonia's big brown eyes widened as she cried out, "That was the day of the murder! What are you implying?"

"It is a formality, but I have to ask and check out alibis of all people concerned."

A couple walking their dog went by. Antonia waited until after they had passed before she answered, "I was at the same job on Friday two weeks ago as this morning, where I always start at 9 o'clock," and she gave the name and address of that particular client.

"Thank you for your cooperation." And the detective watched her carefully as she continued, "Now that we have that out of the way, are you aware that Mrs. Horton made a legacy in her will to benefit you?"

"A what?" Antonia stammered.

"You are the beneficiary of a substantial amount of money mentioned in her will."

Except for the chirping of a bird in a nearby tree, there was complete silence for several seconds. Then Antonia said, "There must be a mistake. Mrs. Horton had a husband and three kids. I'm sure her money goes to them."

"The bulk of it does go to her family, but she recently added a legacy to her will in your favor. I imagine that Mrs. Horton's estate lawyer will contact you soon."

Stunned, the housekeeper said, "I know she was satisfied with my work and think that she liked me, but I had no idea - -" she broke off, the words failing her.

Campbell was about to end the interview when Antonia cried out, "Mercy! Maybe it was because she knew- -" she stopped again in midsentence.

"Knew what? If you have anything to contribute, you need to speak up now. It's important."

"She had a secret. I promised I wouldn't tell." Antonia paused, then added, "Maybe it's okay to let you know now."

"Whatever it is, it can't hurt her any longer."

So she unburdened herself and started with, "It was at the beginning of the year, maybe January or February, before the pandemic for sure. I was about to vacuum the study when I found Mrs. Horton there, leaning against the bookcase, sobbing. On impulse, although I had never done anything like that before, I went over to her and took her in my arms. That shocked her at first, but then I think she was comforted by it. She calmed down enough to tell me that she'd seen her oncologist the other day and learned that her cancer had come back. You see, she'd had breast cancer before.

"Then she told me how the doctor wanted to start her on treatments and she'd said, no way. She'd had surgery, chemotherapy, and radiation two years ago and wasn't about to go through that all over again. The doctor told her that she had a year to live at most, probably less, without treatment. Then she dried her tears and said, 'I'm going to live the time I have left to the fullest. If needed, I'll take pain medication, but I refuse to go through all that other agony.'"

Antonia took a deep breath and went on, "She told me that she was keeping her condition a secret and made me promise that I wouldn't tell a soul. She didn't want to be treated differently and wasn't looking for pity. Toward the end, she may have had to tell her family, if it became obvious, but until then, she said, there was no reason for anyone to know."

There was sadness in Antonia's eyes now as she stated, "Mrs. Horton wanted to live the remainder of her days to the fullest and then Covid-19 hit. If you ask me, she was cheated twice, big time."

As she drove away from Grant Park, Detective Campbell was in a pensive mood. The interview with the housekeeper had been an eye opener, giving her more perception into the victim's personality. At the same time, it complicated the murder investigation. One thing she was sure of, the inheritance came as a total surprise to Antonia Silva.

CHAPTER 28

On Monday morning, October 5, Detective Campbell decided to drop in on Carole Pedrotti unannounced. She had researched the woman, and her condominium in a residential part of Pasadena was easy to find. Since Pedrotti came by to see Bruce Horton in the afternoon the other day, claiming to be on her way to work, Campbell assumed the grocery store manager worked the late shift. She rang her doorbell at 10:00 a.m., hoping to find her at home.

After the second ring, Carole looked through the peephole and yelled, "Who's there?"

The detective held up her ID and stated, "Lieutenant Claudia Campbell from the Monrovia City Police Department."

"Shit," Carole mumbled to herself. Aloud she said, "Hold on," and went to grab her robe, donning it over her see-through negligée.

When she finally opened the door, it was evident that the woman hadn't been up for long. Her hair was a mess and there was sleep in the corner of one of her eyes.

"Sorry to intrude on you," the detective said. "I'll let you find your mask, then have a few questions. I won't take up much of your time."

"Come on in then and have a seat," said Carole, and directed the detective to the living room.

The sound of a whistling kettle came from the kitchen. Carole rushed to silence it, then hollered from there, "Want some coffee?"

"No, thanks," Campbell replied, observing her surroundings. The spacious room was furnished with two upholstered chairs and a sofa, facing a big screen TV. There was a small bookcase against one wall, holding two rows of hardcover editions, and an upright piano by another. There was only one framed picture in the entire room. It was a nude oil on canvas. The detective sat down on one of the chairs and waited.

When Carole reappeared, she wore a mask and carried a mug with instant coffee, saying, "Don't mind if I have mine? I can't function without it in the morning."

"No problem."

Carole plopped herself down on the sofa's edge, the farthest away from the other, and went right into attack mode, saying, "I assume you're here because of Cecile Horton's murder. I know nothing about it. Heck, I didn't even know the woman!"

"You know her husband well, though."

"I know him, but hardly well. We went to high school together."

"Come now, Ms. Pedrotti, I'm aware that you were intimate with Mr. Horton. And I'm not talking back in high school. The two of you had an affair much more recently than that."

"Who says so?" Carole demanded, her eyes full of challenge.

"Mr. Horton told me."

Carole's emotions went from surprise to hurt from the betrayal to anger, all in a split second. She hissed, "The bastard!"

In another second she had herself in control again, lifted her mask, took a sip of coffee, and then said, "That still doesn't change the fact that I didn't know Cecile and certainly had no cause to strangle her."

"So you don't mind telling me where you were on Friday, September 18, from 8:45 a.m. until 10:00 a.m.?"

"Same place as we are right now," she said. "I've been working the late shift for the last several months and as you can tell, I'm not an early riser."

"Do you have someone who can verify that?"

Carole stamped her foot and said, "Obviously not! I live alone. You just have to take my word for it."

She did not even try to disguise her hostility as she jumped off the sofa and scowled, "If that is all, I'd like to take a shower now."

Campbell got to her feet as well and said, "Yes, Ms. Pedrotti, that's all," and walked out of the living room to the hallway, then led herself out the door. She heard the lock being switched closed behind her with a thud.

CHAPTER 29

Campbell could not just take the housekeeper's word about what she had learned concerning the victim's illness. She needed to have it confirmed. It took a bit of finesse on her part, but she got Cecile's oncologist's name and contact information in the end.

When she called Bruce Horton, his first words were, "Have you caught my wife's killer?" Instead of a straight answer, she told him she was looking into the victim's medical history and asked him to provide her with the name of Cecile's cancer specialist.

He was reluctant, at first, protesting, "What the hell has her medical history got to do with her murder?"

After explaining that she needed to have insight into all of the victim's aspects of life, he gave in. He did not recall the oncologist's name but gave her the name and contact information of Cecile's surgeon. Through said surgeon's office, she was directed to the oncologist, Dr. Norma Wong, who agreed to speak with her for ten minutes, squeezing her in between patients, on Tuesday afternoon.

At the appropriate day and time, Campbell was standing outside of that office, waiting in line to get in. Only three patients were allowed to sit in the waiting room at the same time. The queue moved relatively fast, as several doctors shared the same offices.

Once inside, she barely gave the generic waiting room décor a glance and focused on the people. Seated a distance away from her was a bald young woman who had gone through chemo recently. A frail old man sat near the door to the examining rooms, holding on to his cane with both hands. It occurred to her that this was an entirely different scene than she had experienced in the waiting area at the Law Offices of Stolzerman, Blyte & Morales. Coronavirus or not, cancer happened, and she could imagine that despite the availability of virtual telemedicine, treating these patients in person was still the best way to go.

When it was the detective's turn, a nurse ushered her into Dr. Wong's office. The doctor was a petite Asian woman, professional and organized. She had an open file with Cecile Long-Horton's record in front of her and came straight to the point.

She stated, "Under the circumstances, I'm not breaking any doctor/patient confidentiality. Mrs. Horton came to us at the end of January, complaining of pain in the spine. Considering her history of breast cancer two years prior, I ordered bloodwork, a bone scan, and an MRI. The result came back positive for bone metastasis."

"What does that mean?"

"She had metastatic breast cancer, meaning that her cancer came back and had traveled to the bones." Dr. Wong continued, "There is no cure, but we can prolong life. I recommended aggressive treatment that may have given her severe side effects and reduced her quality of life. Mrs. Horton refused treatment. I warned her that the pain would get worse and eventually become unbearable. She replied that she'd deal with it.

"I told her to at least think it over and give me a call if she had a change of heart. A few days later, she did call but not because she had changed her mind. She was as determined as ever to reject treatment. She contacted me with the request not to tell her family, or anyone else, about her condition. I assured her that her record was confidential, and even without her asking, my staff and I would never give out information about its content. However, I offered to get her in touch with a support group, which she turned down."

"How long did you expect her to live?"

"Without treatment, which was her choice, a maximum of a year, probably less," said the doctor. Then she checked the time and Campbell knew her ten minutes were up.

CHAPTER 30

Rather than a regular phone call, Campbell and Sprint opted for a Facetime session that evening. The detective took extra care with adding mascara and lipstick before she dialed.

"What a treat for sore eyes," he said. "You look fantastic, Claudia!"

"Thanks. And you look like your healthy self again. When are you coming back?"

"My quarantine is over tomorrow, so maybe we'll run into each other at the department."

Campbell got down to business and stated, "I talked with two new suspects," and she described her interviews with Antonia Silva and Carole Pedrotti.

He paid keen attention and then said, "Does knowing of the victim's terminal illness change the way you're looking at the investigation?"

"It came as a shock, and at first I thought that I needed to look at things differently, but now I'm convinced that it doesn't change anything."

"I agree," he said. "Suicide is out of the question; it's practically impossible to strangle oneself. As for assisted suicide, there are more civilized ways to do it than wringing someone's neck." He wiggled his pointer for emphasis and added, "And if someone decided on their own to put her out of her misery, that too could have been done with a simple pill or two."

"I doubt that she was even in any severe pain yet, and don't forget, except for the housekeeper, nobody knew of her condition."

"She seemed to be a secretive sort of a woman."

Campbell stated, "I knew that already when her husband told me he didn't have the estate lawyers' info. Then later, it became clear to me why he was left in the dark. Bruce Horton does not inherit, according to the victim's will."

"That *is* strange. It leaves him without a motive, though. At least where money is concerned. Having her alive and supporting him financially was in his best interest. Too bad, normally we look at spouses as the most likely suspects."

"In Bruce Horton's case there is also the physical evidence. According to the coroner, Cecile died around 9:00 a.m. but not before. Her husband was at the dentist's at 9 o'clock on the day of the homicide. His alibi is confirmed." Campbell added, "On the other hand, he did have an affair."

With a grin Sprint said, "Affairs rarely lead to murder." Then he changed gear and asked, "How big is that legacy in favor of the housekeeper?"

"I don't know, but the lawyer said it was a substantial sum."

"What impression did you have of her?"

"Antonia Silva struck me as a hardworking, kind, and loyal woman. That she grieved for her employer was obvious, and the news about the legacy took her by complete surprise. Unless, of course, she is a terrific actor."

"I take it that you checked out the housekeeper's claim about the victim's medical condition?"

"Affirmative. I talked with her oncologist, Dr. Norma Wong, earlier today who confirmed Mrs. Long-Horton's diagnosis of metastatic breast cancer. According to Dr. Wong, she had less than a year to live."

"Now, Claudia, tell me your impression of the Pedritti woman."

"It's Pedrotti. Carole Pedrotti is arrogant and sure of what she wants. Although no longer young, she is definitely good-looking. I saw her when she most likely just got out of bed, and she managed to come across as above average attractive. Not only that, but I got the feeling that men could easily get under her spell, if you know what I mean.

"She didn't seem afraid of me nor the investigation and got hostile when she couldn't come up with an alibi. She practically threw me out of her place!"

Sprint laughed and remarked, "I'd love to have seen that!"

"Don't get cocky. Anyhow, you wanted to get my impression of Bruce Horton's lover. Sometimes a person's character comes through loud and clear when one studies their surroundings."

"How do you mean?"

"There is a portrait of a nude hanging on her living room wall. I recognized the model. It is none other than Carole Pedrotti herself."

"I see. She's also a bit of a narcissist."

Then he asked, "Have you figured out the 'bad apple' remark the victim made?"

"I still have no clue about that. If I knew who and what she meant by it, I could tackle that person. As it stands, I have to go by elimination, and so far, I haven't been able to eliminate anyone. Not even by the murder weapon."

"What murder weapon?"

Claudia stated, "All the suspects I've interviewed, male and female alike, have big, strong hands."

"I get what you mean now. Don't be discouraged. You're good at your job and will figure it out." And before they disconnected, he said, "I can't wait to see you in person."

Claudia couldn't deny that Sprint's last remark gave her an unexpected thrill.

CHAPTER 31

Detective Campbell decided to let the family members know what she had learned about Cecile's health prior to her homicide and asked for another Zoom session. Besides feeling they had a right to know, she also had an ulterior motive for doing so. By watching each person's reaction when springing that bit of news, she hoped to get further in her investigation. The meeting was scheduled for Wednesday morning, October 7, and she had asked for the siblings' spouses to also be present, if possible. Everyone had logged on, except for Mateo, Julie's husband, who was installing a new air-conditioning system at a client's residence.

Before anyone could inquire how the case was coming along, Campbell got straight to the point and informed them of the victim's metastatic breast cancer which had spread to her bones. Everyone seemed to be in total shock, but each person's response was different.

Darrell was the first to comment, asking, "Who told you that?"

"Your mother confided in Antonia Silva."

Julie jumped in with, "Antonia must have made that up. Mom wasn't sick."

"Her physician confirmed the fact and told me that as of January of this year, Mrs. Horton had less than a year to live."

Bruce shook his head and addressed the detective with, "That can't be. Cecile was fit; she vigorously exercised every day."

"That might explain why her pain had not been severe yet and she was able to keep her condition a secret. Check with Dr. Norma Wong, your wife's oncologist, who will confirm that her illness and suffering was about to progress rapidly."

Darrell burst out, "That explains why she became such a softy lately. So it wasn't because of the pandemic. She knew that she was doomed."

Sybille, who looked in over Darrell's shoulder, remarked, "She was lucky to come to a quick end, being spared a prolonged painful sickness."

Jason yelled, "How dare you say Mom was lucky to get murdered!"

"Just telling it like it is," the former said with a smirk.

Candy did not comment but covered Jason's shaking hands with her own, trying to calm him as he continued, "I can't believe Mom revealed her illness to the housekeeper and not her own family. That's an insult."

Detective Campbell said, "I believe that Mrs. Horton wanted to avoid being pitied and may have also tried to shield you all from worry." She went on, "I thought that you would take comfort knowing that your loved one's days were limited to begin with, but maybe I was wrong in that assumption."

Candy spoke for the first time and stated, "I don't know about the rest of you, but as far as I'm concerned, Cecile's withholding her state of health from us showed dignity and consideration."

Then she looked in the direction of the detective's square and asked, "How is your investigation coming along?"

"I'm making progress," Campbell replied, and the meeting came to an end.

That was a lie. She had some ideas, but "progress" was wishful thinking.

CHAPTER 32

Raul Ibarra got up early on Thursday morning. He needed to do some dusting and straightening up of his rental bungalow in San Fernando before leaving for the gardening job in La Cañada Flintridge. While carefully dusting off his treasured bronzes, he reminisced about his life. At 68, and a widower of many years, he was looking forward to retirement and a life of leisure in his native Guadalajara in Central Mexico.

As a young man he had immigrated to the United States with his parents and first worked in a factory and then many decades ago started his gardening business. By word of mouth and known for doing an excellent job, he had established a wide clientele, all up and down the San Fernando Valley and San Gabriel Valley. He lived a frugal lifestyle and had been able to accumulate a small nest egg over the years.

With his wife gone and his kids and grandkids no longer depending on him, he was confident he'd be able to live out his golden years in comfort in Guadalajara, where he still had relatives. He had worked hard his entire life and admitted to himself he had grown tired. It would be fun to relax a bit, and he indulged in the vision of swinging in a hammock, tied between two palm trees, sipping Tequila. As soon as it was safe to travel again, he'd give his vast clientele notice and prepare to make the big move.

Then he thought back to Mrs. Horton's funeral, exactly one week ago. Working for that lady had been one of his longest jobs, stretching over decades, way before she'd married Mr. Horton. He'd known her as Mrs. Long then. Poor Lady! He tried not to dwell on how he and the young woman had found her, laying in a heap at her own doorstep. But he was glad he'd had the courage to question the person about what he'd seen when he got to the house earlier that day. Now that it had been explained to him, he could ban the incident from his mind.

As he draped the feather duster over the *Girl on a Swing*, one of his favorite bronzes, he reminisced on his bronze statues collection. The acquiring of bronzes had started with a wounded warrior riding on a horse, called *End of Trail*, that he'd run across at a swap meet, followed by more Western riders. Soon, the bronze bug had hit him and he'd amassed different kinds of statues he could afford, going to swap meets and auctions. The collection grew to about twenty pieces he displayed in every room of his small house. They varied in size, from the smallest of only five inches, to the tallest of over twenty inches.

He sighed. Too bad he couldn't take the bronzes with him when he moved. A few were crafted by well-known artists, such as Remington, and were titled, but most were nameless and created by unknown sculptors. He had mentioned the collection during the gathering in the Hortons' back patio after the funeral, and by pure luck, someone interested in purchasing it was scheduled to come have a look at noon today. He sure hoped they would reach a deal, and his treasures would find a new home.

Raul's second job of the morning was in Pasadena, and he was planning to come home for lunch before heading out to clients closer to his house. So showing off his bronzes at noon was perfect.

It was time to leave for his job in La Cañada Flintridge. He returned the vacuum cleaner and duster to the utility closet and had one last look around. The house was now clean and ready for company, he determined.

***

When Raul got back at noon, the prospective buyer of his collection was already in front of his house.

He parked his truck on the driveway and went to greet his guest, saying, "I hope I didn't make you wait long. Let's go inside. How about some lunch first?"

The person replied, "I got here barely a minute ago myself. And thanks for the offer, but my time is limited, I'm on my way to another engagement and have only a few minutes to look at the bronzes."

They walked along the driveway towards the front door, when the individual suddenly stood still and said, "Do you smell it?"

Raul asked, "Smell what?"

"There's a distinct smell of gasoline."

They hurried back to the truck and sniffed, but there was no odor around the vehicle.

"I think it's coming from your shed."

"You're right," said Raul, suddenly alarmed, and he ran toward the shed, located next to the side of the house, with his guest close on his heels.

There was no mistaking the strong smell as Raul opened the shed's door. He raced inside and slipped and fell when he stepped onto the puddle of gasoline that had accumulated on the floor. He suppressed a scream as he felt a sharp pain in his ankle.

Before he could recover from the shock of the fall and try to scramble back onto his feet, the person behind him stood by the open door and said, "Sorry, but you've seen too much."

In the next split second, the villain lit an entire matchbook, tossed it inside, and then closed the shed's door, jamming a wedge under it from the outside.

The culprit was already back on the street and started the car when the big bang of the explosion sounded.

CHAPTER 33

Jason and Candy sat side by side on the sofa, watching the late news on that Thursday. There was a segment about someone overdosing on opioids.

Candy turned to her husband and said, "You *are* getting help, right?"

"Sure," he said, "as soon as it's safe to see someone."

With her eyes kept on the screen she said, "You could do so right now. I've researched it. There is one-on-one online therapy available, and group sessions are also offered."

"You had no business looking into that stuff. I'll do my own research when I'm good and ready. So back off!" he yelled.

He was about to storm out of the room when Candy held him back, pointing at the newscaster on TV who was in mid-sentence "- - *burning down the shed at the residence. Sadly, the firefighters couldn't save Raul Ibarra, who perished inside, but - -*"

"Oh no! Did you hear? That's your mom's gardener who perished in the fire," she shrieked.

"We don't know that for sure. Could be someone else."

"How many Raul Ibarra's do you think live in San Fernando? Of course it's him. Poor man, burning to death must be one of the most painful ways to die."

Then she said, "It's past 11 o'clock, too late now, but we'll call your brother and sister tomorrow so we can all decide what to do."

"What the heck are you talking about?"

She stared at him for a few seconds and then said, "You honestly don't know?"

He shook his head.

"It stands to reason that Mr. Ibarra's death and Cecile's are connected."

"You're out of your mind!"

"Apply logic, Jason. Coincidences like that don't happen." And she added, "I'm starting to get afraid for ourselves. Maybe instead of calling your siblings, we should let Detective Campbell know."

Jason said, "Don't you dare! The anchor didn't say Ibarra was murdered. The burning down of his shed may have been an accident and nothing more. So don't stick your nose in. And don't call Darrell and Julie either. If the news was about the gardener we know - - and it may well be a different Raul Ibarra, the name is common in the Latino community - - they'll find out soon enough."

A similar conversation went on in San Marino at Darrell and Sybille's residence. They had also watched the 11 o'clock news and, after some debating, opted to keep silent about it as well.

Julie and Mateo Martinez, on the other hand, were already fast asleep at that time and were spared the news, at least for the moment.

CHAPTER 34

Claudia and Sprint faced one another across the table at a restaurant in charming Old Town Monrovia on Saturday evening, October 10. The weather was still mild enough to enjoy outdoor dining.

Sprint asked, "Is this a date or are you using me as a sounding board again?"

Claudia winked at him and replied, "A little of both." Then she got serious and said, "About the Cecile Long-Horton case. I called another Zoom meeting with all suspects, sprang the victim's terminal illness on them and looked for their reactions."

"And?"

"As expected, it was a shock to them all, but, unless I read it wrong, one person probably thought, 'I could have spared myself the trouble.'"

"Which one?"

"I'm keeping that to myself for now since I could be wrong."

A masked couple strolled by on the sidewalk and she remarked, "We're so used to seeing everyone with half their faces covered that we hardly notice it any longer."

Then she got back to what really was utmost on her mind and said, "Did you hear about the fire in San

Fernando, where a man burned to death inside his own shed?"

"I didn't, but that's a terrible way to go. What happened?"

Claudia said, "It was on Thursday night's news. There was an explosion inside the shed and the poor man couldn't get out and was overwhelmed by the flames. They mentioned his name, Raul Ibarra, and I knew I'd come across that name recently, but couldn't remember where or how. It didn't leave me any peace.

"This morning, I finally remembered and flipped through the initial report of the first responders who had interviewed the grocery delivery person and the gardener. The two had found Cecile Long-Horton's corps. Sure enough, the gardener's name was Raul Ibarra, residing in San Fernando."

"That can't be a coincidence," said Sprint.

"I'd bet my last dollar that it's not." She sighed and continued, "According to the young woman and the gardener's statements, which I read when I was assigned to this case, there was no reason for me to interview either one of them again. They came upon the body about an hour after its demise and couldn't shed light on the case. Or so I thought. Now I could kick myself for not having spoken to the gardener in person!

"He must have known or seen something important that caused the murderer to feel threatened and resort to eliminate him. Had I taken the time to interview Mr. Ibarra myself, I may have been able to prevent his death."

"Don't torment yourself. He probably wouldn't have told you about it, if indeed he knew something important. Whatever it was, the man must have shrugged it off as irrelevant, or he would have enlightened the first responders."

Claudia mumbled, more to herself than to Sprint, "But it's strange that the criminal waited three weeks after the murder to act."

She tried to shake the guilty feeling, then stated, "I talked to the person in charge of the shed explosion investigation at the San Fernando Police Department today. The forensic experts determined that arson is definitely the case and they've launched a homicide investigation into Raul Ibarra's death. The good news is that the firefighters, although not able to save the gardener's life while the shed burned to the ground, were in time to stop the flames from reaching the house."

Sprint asked, "So what's your plan?"

"I'm going to investigate the fire myself but have to be careful not to step on anyone's toes. As you well know, San Fernando is not in our jurisdiction."

Sprint paid for the meal, and before they got up to leave he remarked, "Once the current mess is behind us, I'll take you on a date with all the bells and whistles."

"Does that mean flowers, dinner at the Wolfgang Puck restaurant, and a theater show?"

"For starters!"

CHAPTER 35

It was only 8:30 when Campbell got home, not too late to call Bruce Horton.

He picked up right away and she said, "I'm so sorry about your gardener, Raul Ibarra."

"Sorry about what?"

"Oh, you don't know," she said, and relayed the bad news.

"How awful! How did it happen?"

"I don't know the details yet, but it looks like the work of an arsonist and there is a homicide investigation."

"A what? Oh no! Not again."

She gave him time to digest that and then said, "The reason I'm calling is to ask how long Raul Ibarra had been in your employ?"

"Let me think. He's always taken care of our yard, but I don't know when Cecile first hired him. He was her gardener long before we were married. Her sons and daughter may remember the year he started working for her." And he asked, "Is it important?"

"Not at all. I'm just trying to get a clear picture of the man."

Before they ended the call Bruce asked, "How is your investigation of Cecile's murder coming along?"

"I'm getting closer to the truth every day," was her reply.

***

Campbell then made her next call. She didn't know why she chose to talk with Julie and not one of the sons. Possibly because she wanted to know more about the woman herself, not only the information she was seeking about the gardener.

Julie had also been in the dark about what had happened to Raul. When the detective sprang the news on her, she was devastated.

After the initial shock, the tears welled up and she burst out, "He was trapped inside his shed when there was an explosion, you said?"

"I didn't say that he was trapped but that's what must have happened."

"He was such a nice man!"

"You knew him well?"

"Well enough."

"The reason I'm calling is to get an idea of how long he had been your mother's gardener."

"I remember Mr. Ibarra coming to take care of our lawn and garden as far back as when I was in the first grade. I'm 44 now. That should give you an idea."

Campbell did the math and then commented, "38 years is a long time. The work relationship must have been satisfactory on both sides."

"Sure. He was an excellent gardener and I can imagine that Mom paid him well." And she reminisced, "In my primary school years, I was always pleased if I happened to be home when he showed up. Before we had the pool, there was a big flower garden in our backyard. Mr. Ibarra let me have my own small area where I could grow whatever I wanted. He showed me how to prepare the soil and taught me how to plant from either seeds or starter plants, according to season.

"Even in my awkward teens, he had kind words for me. As an adult, the times we both happened to be at Mom's house at the same time were rare, but he always had a welcoming smile." She sighed and uttered, "I'm having a hard time accepting what happened to him."

The detective asked, "When was the last time you saw Mr. Ibarra?"

"At Mom's funeral. That shows you how close to our family he was. Due to the pandemic, the number of people who could attend was limited. Mr. Ibarra and Antonia Silva, Mom's housekeeper, were the only non-family members present."

"Ah yes, Antonia Silva. What do you think of her?"

"I believe she is a competent housekeeper."

"I meant personally."

"She seemed devoted to Mom, judging by all the tears she shed at the funeral."

Campbell sensed a sore spot there and went for it, asking, "Would it surprise you to learn that there is a legacy in favor of Antonia Silva in your mother's will?"

"No, I'm not surprised."

And without warning, a torrent of angry words came out of Julie's mouth. "It stands to reason that the two must have had a good relationship with one another. How else would Mom have confided in her and not the family about being terminally ill? I mean, informing the housekeeper, but not her own flesh and blood, that she had only months to live, what does that tell you? I'm sure she'd have preferred perfect, slim, little Antonia as a daughter over me."

Embarrassed of having dumped her feelings on the detective, Julie changed the subject and asked, "Are you investigating Mr. Ibarra's death?"

"San Fernando is not my jurisdiction, but I'll try to give their authorities a helping hand."

Julie stared at the phone after hanging up and thought, what on earth possessed me to tell the cop all that? The woman caught me off guard, that's why.

Detective Campbell was thinking, it's obvious that Julie realizes that Ibarra's death was also a homicide and that the two crimes are connected. Why else would she assume that I'd investigate the gardener's death?

CHAPTER 36

Mid-morning on Sunday, Campbell was on her way to San Fernando. During the half-hour drive she reviewed the facts she had obtained from the local police officer. Of course, before he disclosed any information, she had to explain why she was interested in the gardener's case. When she mentioned that she was investigating the murder of one of Ibarra's clients and thought the two crimes may be related, the officer in charge opened up.

According to the San Fernando authorities, 68-year-old Raul Ibarra had lived alone in his rental bungalow. On Thursday, October 8, there was an explosion in the shed next to his house. An anonymous person called 911 at 12:08 p.m. and reported the fire. The caller had not been identified, and it was suspected that the individual happened to drive by Ibarra's residence at that time and saw the smoke and flames. The firefighters got there within minutes but could not save Raul Ibarra's life or the shed. It burned to the ground but they contained the fire before it reached the house.

They found Ibarra's charred body, barely recognizable, among the rubble. Although nothing was left of the wooden shed itself, a metal gasoline canister was found at the scene. The forensic investigators determined that deliberate arson was the cause of the explosion and consequently the fire.

The San Fernando officer she'd talked to remarked that suicide did not come into play; nobody would torch themselves to death. As a result, a homicide investigation was under way. He also stated that so far, talking with neighbors had been fruitless. It appeared that nobody had seen anything suspicious.

They left their conversation with the promise of sharing their findings with each other. Whether or not it would be put to practice remained to be seen. After all, neither had jurisdiction in the other's territory.

Then she thought back to the conversation she had had with the young woman who had delivered groceries to the Horton residence on the day of Cecile Long-Horton's homicide. After she'd learned what had happened to the gardener, she wanted to make sure that there wouldn't be another killing she may be able to prevent. The young woman assured her she hadn't seen anything suspicious or out of the ordinary on that day.

The young woman also stated that she had not known anyone at the Horton residence and that it was the first time she had been at their house, just making a delivery to the address she had been given. The gardener told her that the body they came upon was the residence owner's. Otherwise, she would not have known even that. She ended their talk by saying that finding Cecile's body had traumatized her and she was trying hard to forget the ghastly experience.

At this point of her musing, Detective Campbell had arrived at her destination and surveyed the area.

The late Mr. Ibarra's bungalow was in a residential neighborhood of mostly single family houses, either rented or owned, with a few apartment complexes thrown in. The detective parked on the street and then walked down the driveway.

There was no yellow crime tape, an indication that the forensic team and their photographer were done with their job. It was obvious where the shed had been. Instead of the structure, she came upon burned debris and a blackened ground. Campbell was certain that there was no longer anything for her to explore at the scene. Whatever evidence there was, must have long been collected by the forensic crew.

The detective looked over to the next-door neighbors' house. Yes, she determined, from two of their windows people had a clear view to where the shed had stood. She turned around, walked back up the driveway, and then made a beeline toward that house next door.

CHAPTER 37

Raul's neighbor had a hard time coping. The restrictions of life during the pandemic always hit the woman hardest on Sundays. Not being allowed to attend Sunday Mass in person was something she missed beyond words. Watching it on TV didn't come close to the experience. Lately she'd been praying a lot for her two friends who were in the hospital with Covid-19, but she'd have liked to light a candle for each at the church.

As far as her family's means of income, her husband was still holding down his job as meat cutter at their local grocery store, but she herself was unemployed. People who owned the hair salon she had worked for had barely held it together until they were permitted to reopen for a brief period in June. However, they could not withstand the second closing of their doors. By the time the green light was given to reopen salons again in September, it was too late. The place had not survived.

She thought, thank God our two eldest are on their own and we only have to support a teenage boy. He is the smartest of our kids, and we'd hoped to send him to college. Now I doubt that we'll be able to afford it. Worrying about money seemed a constant nag at the back of her mind, now that she had plenty of time to brood.

She worried too about catching Covid. She herself was careful, always wearing a mask and keeping her distance from people, but her husband and son were not that strict. Her boy, especially, sneaked out to hang with his friends, every chance he got. On the other hand, getting out of the house and catching some fresh air was better for him than playing video games all day long.

Just as that thought crossed her mind, the doorbell rang.

***

There was mistrust in the neighbor's eyes when she opened the door halfway.

The detective held up her I.D. and said, "Sorry to bother you on a Sunday. I'm Lieutenant Campbell from the Monrovia City Police Department. I'm looking into the explosion that happened at Mr. Ibarra's shed."

The woman eyed her with undisguised hostility now and said, "The police were already here the other day. I told them that I know nothing and am telling you now, *I know nothing.*"

"I believe you. I just have a few general questions about your neighbor, Mr. Ibarra. May I come in?"

The lady of the house looked up and down the street and then asked, "Where's your car?"

Campbell pointed to where it was parked.

"Good, it's not a police car. I don't like people to think we have police business. Okay then, come in," she said, and opened the door wide to let the detective step inside.

Once in the living room, the woman did not offer the detective a seat but glared at her with apprehension. And before the other could start the inquiry, she said, "From Monrovia, you say. So what are you doing here?"

"Excellent question. I'm investigating a case that may be tied to what happened to Mr. Ibarra."

"Raul wouldn't hurt a fly. So stop investigating him!"

"You knew him well?"

"We've been neighbors for many years. We didn't socialize much, but he was a good man."

"So you would want justice for him, right?"

"What makes you sure someone torched his shed?" the woman replied. "Chances are that he was careless with something flammable he stored in his shed, and poof, it went up in flames."

Campbell said, "That's why we're examining the matter. If you by chance saw any stranger on Mr. Ibarra's property last Thursday, please say so."

"I told you before, I know nothing and saw nothing."

The detective glanced at the woman's hand and noticed the wedding ring. She said, "Is your husband available? He may have seen something."

"He's not home right now," the other replied and thought, I'm not going to tell her that he's kicking a soccer ball around with his male friends. That might be against the law because of Covid. Aloud she added, "And anyhow, he was at work on Thursday."

"But you were home?"

"Sure," the woman admitted, "but I mind my own business and don't spy on my neighbors."

"You heard the explosion, though?"

"Even with my vacuum cleaner on, I heard the bang. I didn't know where it came from at first but soon afterward, the fire engines made another racket and stopped right at the top of Raul's driveway."

The woman continued, "I've told this already to the local police. I'm sorry I can't help you," and it was clear that she wanted the detective to leave.

At that moment her 15-year-old son, who had been listening in the hallway, stepped into the living room and said, "I saw something suspicious."

As he came closer, his mother nudged him with her elbow and said, "No, you didn't! Don't make things up."

Campbell said, "I'd like to hear your account of what you saw."

So the teen complied. "It was toward the end of my morning class. I hate the online schooling. Some students didn't get it, and the math teacher repeated and explained the entire process of solving an equation all over again. I was bored and looked out the window. I saw someone walk down Mr. Ibarra's driveway, carrying a container. The person stopped at the shed and went inside, then came out again without the container.

"At first I thought that was weird, but when I thought more about it, I decided that the person must have made some kind of a gardening delivery and Mr. Ibarra had told him to put it in the shed. Then the morning class ended and I forgot all about it."

Campbell asked, "At what time did your class end?"

"Ten to 12:00."

"Did you also happen to look out the window before or during the explosion?"

The boy shook his head and said, "I missed the whole show since I was riding my bike to meet up with my friend. I heard the firefighter's siren, though, and when I realized they were heading down our street, I turned around and came back home. There is a fire hydrant right in front of our house and I watched from the street as they sprayed the burning shed."

"Did you just now think of the person you saw that day?"

He looked at his mom, torn between answering truthfully or earning her wrath. The truth won and he said, "Actually, I thought of it later that day."

"Did you mention it to the San Fernando Police Officers?"

"I never talked to them."

"Would you be able to recognize the individual?" Campbell asked.

"Probably not." He grinned and added, "All Gringos look the same to me. This one was wearing shorts, a polo shirt, and a cap, ready for the golf course."

His mom gave him another nudge, then turned to the detective and said, "He's making it all up to feel important. I think you should leave now."

CHAPTER 38

As soon as Detective Campbell was out the door, the woman turned to her son and reprimanded him in a torrent of rapid Spanish, "What's the matter with you? Fibbing to the police! Don't you know that could have serious consequences? I tried to stop you but you had to show off and make up a tall-tale."

"I swear it's true. I saw the person go in and out of the shed."

"So why didn't you say so before now?"

"Because I knew what Dad's and your reaction would be. *None of our business. We don't talk to cops* is your attitude."

"That's right. Even if you did see a stranger; we don't blab to the police." And she added, "But you had no business being disrespectful."

"What?"

"That thing you said about Gringos was mean."

"Oh that. It was only a joke and she didn't seem to mind. I saw her crack a smile."

"What were you doing looking out the window in the first place, instead of paying attention to your teacher? I'm surprised you're still getting good grades despite goofing off."

The boy suppressed the smart aleck reply he had on his tongue. In the mood his mom was in, ever since the woman cop had entered their house, she might ground him for good if he wasn't careful.

His mother continued, "There isn't much punishment I can give you these days, but if you don't shape up, I'll take your computer away and only hand it back for schooling and homework. All those video games are bad for you."

Mulling over what happened next door once more, he asked, "So what do you think old Señor Ibarra did in Monrovia that made somebody bump him off?"

"Watch your language, boy!" And after a pause she answered his question by stating, "I have no idea and don't want to know. Besides, as I told the policewoman, he may not have been killed on purpose. It could have been an accident."

The teen thought, she doesn't believe that for a minute, but knew better than to voice his thought out loud.

CHAPTER 39

On her return drive to Monrovia, Campbell considered what she had learned. She was convinced that the boy had told the truth, despite his mother's insistence that he had made the whole thing up. She also thought that his statement of not being able to recognize the culprit was correct. The first neighbor's window facing Raul Ibarra's driveway was from their living room. So the other must be looking out from the teen's bedroom, she deduced. And at that angle, he would have only seen the person from the side and back.

The boy didn't say that it was a man he saw, so it could have been a woman. The weather was still warm; plenty of women walked around in shorts and a polo shirt. Too bad the teen did not stick around to see the entire drama.

What does the boy's account amount to for me? Campbell reflected. I have to reconstruct the events as best I can. Timing seems to be a crucial factor. A minute or so before the witness's class ended at 11:50 a.m., the culprit walked down the driveway, carrying a container, and vanished into the shed. Seconds later, he left the shed without the container. Since the boy did not mention that he saw Raul Ibarra on his property at that time, I have to assume that he was not home yet. So logic dictates that the stranger was setting the stage minutes before Ibarra showed up.

The detective knew the information she'd obtained from the San Fernando authorities by heart. There had been evidence of a metal gasoline canister at the scene. The fire was reported at 12:08 p.m. She thought, those are the facts. From them I deduce that the so-called stranger must have had a rendezvous with Ibarra at his house but was no stranger at all. The culprit would have gotten there early, poured a can of gasoline over the inside of the shed, and then waited for his prey. When Ibarra arrived, the two either had business to attend to in the shed, or the killer lured him to it. That the owner of the shed would enter first makes sense. Lighting a match and tossing it in after poor Mr. Ibarra, was child's play.

Someone had mentioned that he was trapped inside the shed. Now who made that comment? That must have been precisely what had happened. She assumed that after setting the place on fire, the culprit in some way blocked the door from the outside. By the time the firefighters arrived, he or she was long gone.

This killer acted without mercy, and took chances. Both murders were committed in broad daylight and executed on the spot. It must have only taken a couple of minutes to strangle the first victim, and the torching of the shed involved a bit of preparation but was also carried out swiftly.

As the guilt about not having interviewed Raul Ibarra herself - - which may have avoided his killing - - entered her mind once more, the detective swore that she would avenge his death.

CHAPTER 40

Once again Detective Campbell mulled over the fact that the killer had waited three weeks before silencing Mr. Ibarra.

She was at practice at the shooting range on Monday morning. As a rule, wearing earmuffs and safety glasses enabled her to concentrate fully on her task. Not so this time. The Ibarra question constantly nagged at the back of her mind. On average she was a good shot, but on that Monday her performance was poor. None of her rounds made it even close to the bullseye. They landed around the outer rings of the target. One shot missed the target altogether.

She was about to reload and stopped in mid-action as it hit her. Of course, she told herself. The funeral was on October 1. At that event Ibarra must have mentioned something that was dangerous to the culprit. The man either witnessed or knew something about Cecile's murder. He may not have been aware of what that something meant, or that he had incriminating evidence. To the villain, however, it must have been enough of a threat to provoke action.

The gardener was killed on October 8, so it took the murderer a week to plan the details and execute the deed. That makes complete sense, Campbell deduced. Too bad that I can't narrow it down, since all my suspects attended the funeral. This means that I need to interview everyone again, perhaps only with a phone call, as I'm basically checking for alibis in the second homicide.

With this minor problem solved, the detective was now able to concentrate on her shooting and came nearer the bullseye mark with her last round.

CHAPTER 41

In the next few days Campbell was busy interviewing her suspects for a second time. Some had verifiable alibis while others did not. This time Julie's whereabouts on October 8, the day Raul Ibarra was killed, were confirmed. Several of her employees declared that she was at the El Monte plant from 9:00 a.m. until 5:30 p.m. Mateo, her husband, had two witnesses attesting that he was at his job before and during the time Ibarra's shed was set on fire. Once more, Darrell and Sybille vouched that they were home together during the crucial time on October 8.

The driving time from Sierra Madre to San Fernando is roughly 30 minutes. So the detective had asked Jason and Candy to account for their time from 11:15 a.m. until 12:30 p.m. and learned that Candy had been home with their children but no outsider could confirm her statement. Jason had played a round of golf on said Thursday. He claimed to have left their house a few minutes before noon and had arrived at the Hansen Dam Golf Course at 12:30 p.m. To confirm his claim, he not only had the golf course attendant's validation but suggested that she should check with Bruce Horton, with whom he'd had a reservation to play.

Antonia Silva always took the day off on Thursdays. She reported staying home on the day in question, enjoying being together with her elderly mother and her teenage kids.

Carole Pedrotti had not attended Cecile's funeral, and if Campbell's theory was correct that Mr. Ibarra had been silenced because of something he revealed on the occasion, that particular suspect would be off the hook. In case she was wrong in her deductions - - or if by chance Bruce Horton had told her of the gardener's remark on the day of the funeral - - she gave the woman a call.

When asked to state where she had been during the critical time on Thursday, October 8, Carole said, "I have no idea where I was. In bed, for all I know. I work the late shift, remember?"

And before the detective got in another word, the woman yelled, "Stop harassing me! I know nothing about Cecile's murder and had never even met her. I've already told you that I've been home and I'm sticking to it. Wait a minute. She was killed on a Friday, so why are you asking about a Thursday now?"

Campbell said, "This new date concerns my investigation of Raul Ibarra's homicide."

"Who is that and what are you talking about?"

"Mr. Ibarra was the gardener attending to the Horton residence. He was killed as a result of being trapped in his shed, which had been set on fire."

"That's awful!"

"Yes. Think again of what you were doing on October 8 from about 11:15 a.m. onward."

Carole was no longer angry and even showed a bit of compassion, stating, "I didn't know the man but I'm sorry. Burning to death must be agony. As to my alibi, I was home at the time you mentioned and stayed put until I left for work at 2:40 in the afternoon."

After a pause she said, "You mentioned investigating a homicide. So it wasn't an accident?"

"There is evidence of foul play."

It was clear that Carole had already made the connection when she stated, "So this poor man's murder is linked to that of Cecile's?"

"You got that right."

After ending the call Campbell thought about what she had learned so far from talking with the suspects. As far as alibis went, some folks seemed to be in the clear and others were not. In the end, it all boiled down to motive. All siblings had an equally strong one: Their income was going to be cut in half. One of them had an extra motive, having to do with that "bad apple" comment their mother had made. The detective deduced that Cecile Long-Horton had issued a threat to one of her offspring, like, *if you don't shape up, I'll expose you.* For solving the crime, it didn't much matter what that apple remark had meant, but rather to whom it was addressed.

As to the rest, all the siblings' spouses had an indirect motive where their finances were concerned. Bruce, the victim's husband, did not inherit according to her will. Her death was in fact a monetary loss for him. The man was having an affair, but the detective doubted it contributed to a motive for murder. In regards to Carole Pedrotti, the only thing the detective could think of was that she may have had a deep hatred for the woman she considered her rival.

Antonia Silva gained financially from the victim's death. According to Eduard Blyte, the estate lawyer, the legacy Mrs. Long-Horton added to her will in the housekeeper's favor was substantial.

Campbell mused, did all this get me any further in solving the crimes? Not as much as I would like, she answered her own question. I do have an idea who the culprit might be but proving it is going to be tricky, if not impossible. For now, concentrating on Mr. Ibarra's homicide is my best bet.

CHAPTER 42

Detective Campbell arranged for a Facetime session with Bruce Horton on Friday, October 16.

Instead of a proper greeting he said, "An entire month has passed since Cecile's death. This had better be about letting me know that you've caught her murderer."

"I'm working on it," she replied. "For now, I'm focused on Raul Ibarra's homicide."

Disappointment showed on Bruce's face as he said, "I see."

"I've interviewed suspects and according to Jason Long, the two of you played golf at the Hansen Dam Golf course on October 8, the day that the gardener was killed."

"That is correct."

"I've already talked with the golf course attendant but since the timing of events is of the utmost importance, I need you to verify Mr. Long's statement as to exact times of your golf rendezvous, including making the appointment and getting there."

"Sure," Bruce said, and gave his account. "Neither one of us had played at the Hansen Dam course before. We'd heard that they had re-landscaped the fairways and serviced the greens to perfection, so we gave the place a try. We made a reservation and got a tee time of 12:30 in the afternoon, and since - - -"

"Who made the reservation?"

"I volunteered."

"Sorry! I won't interrupt any more. Please continue."

"No problem," he said. "Now, where was I? Oh yeah, since the location was new to us, I googled the driving times, which were 30 minutes from Jason's house and 35 minutes from mine to get to the course. We drove in separate cars as he planned to run an errand afterward. I don't know if you play golf, but it's customary to arrive 10 to 15 minutes before tee time and check in at the club's front desk. Jason didn't tell me at what time he left home but I assume you asked him and Candy confirmed it."

The detective nodded.

Bruce continued, "I left my house at 11:40 - - you can check with the pool guy who was there - - and got to the golf course at roughly 12:15. I changed into golf shoes and went to register and get a cart. To my surprise, Jason wasn't there yet. He arrived at 12:30, thinking tee off was at 12:45. So we had to hustle in order not to screw up people's tee times in line behind us."

Campbell asked, "Do you and Jason play golf together often?"

He grinned and replied, "That was actually our first time. He called and suggested that we play a round of golf."

"Mr. Long said you were the one who suggested it."

"Oh, did he? No, it was he. I remember he called on Wednesday, right after our Zoom meeting where you informed us that Cecile had been sick. He said that he had recently started to play again and that it would relax us both and distract from the unpleasant things on our minds."

He continued, "I'm not surprised that he's mixing things up. He wasn't himself that day. First he was confused about the tee time and then he seemed distracted the entire 18 holes. I didn't know his usual game, but on that Thursday, he played lousy."

"That clarifies things. Thanks for your assistance."

Bruce asked, "You never said, but at what time exactly was Raul Ibarra's shed torched?"

"Shortly after 12:00 noon."

"That clears Jason, then. Assuming he came straight from home, he wouldn't have left his house much earlier than 12:00, since he didn't show up at the golf course until 12:30."

"It looks that way," said the detective. And she asked, "Something else. Did you know that your wife left a legacy in her will to benefit Antonia Silva?"

He raised an eyebrow and replied, "That's news to me." And he added, "Good for her!"

The detective did not have the heart to ask him if he also knew that he was not mentioned in her will, and ended the Facetime session.

CHAPTER 43

Detective Campbell sat at her desk at the Monrovia Police Department taking care of paperwork involving other cases, but her heart wasn't in it. Something about the timing of Raul's murder nagged at the back of her mind. She finally shoved the forms aside and concentrated on the notes she had taken during the Facetime with Bruce Horton.

Out of habit, she had checked with the young man who serviced his pool and learned that Bruce had left his house at 11:40, just as he had claimed. As for Jason Long, Candy had confirmed that indeed he left the house around noon. Since the confirmation came from his spouse, it had to be taken with a grain of salt.

Bruce had been correct; the distance from Sierra Madre to Hansen Dam was 26 miles and the driving time 30 minutes, and from Monrovia it was 29 miles and 35 minutes. The driving time from Jason's residence in Sierra Madre to Raul Ibarra's house in San Fernando was also 30 minutes.

She had taken her research a step further and checked the driving time from the gardener's home to the golf course. It was 12 minutes. Taking the neighbor boy's statement at face value, she had calculated that the time Mr. Ibarra's shed was set on fire on Thursday, October 8, was a minute or two past 12 o'clock noon.

According to the golf course attendant, Bruce arrived at 12:15 and Jason at 12:30. If everyone told the truth about the times they left their houses, Jason, and of course Bruce, could not have committed the crime.

Yet, Campbell had thought from the start that the short distance between San Fernando and the golf course at Hansen Dam looked suspicious. Why would people from the San Gabriel Valley drive the distance to Hansen Dam when there are plenty of golf courses in-between? But maybe it was a coincidence, after all. She herself was not a golfer. It was possible that folks who played the sport tried out different courses all over the southland.

Did this put her back to square one? Not exactly. She had made progress in the investigation and had certain ideas. One thing was clear, she was dealing with a cunning murderer.

She was going to tackle the backlog paperwork once again when she looked up and gazed into Sprint's eyes.

"Drop everything and let's go for lunch," he suggested.

"You bet," she said and left her paperwork and notes.

CHAPTER 44

Claudia Campbell did not have much of a private life these days, but she had to eat. Early Monday evening of the next week, she was on her way home from one of her other cases and decided on the spur of the moment to stop at a grocery store in Pasadena rather than her local market in Monrovia.

She planned a dinner of a tossed salad followed by spaghetti and Italian sausage. Pasta and sauce were plentiful in her pantry. All she needed to purchase was a head of lettuce, sausage, and a bottle of Cabernet Sauvignon. She grabbed a basket and headed over to the produce, then the meat department and the liquor aisle. After selecting the wine and making her way toward the checkout counter, she witnessed a commotion near the front entrance.

A man without a mask was in a verbal dispute with a clerk and the argument became heated.

He said, "I told you, I just need a couple of items."

The clerk insisted, "Not without a mask!"

The man tried to walk past the irate employee, but she pushed a cart between them, blocking the man's way. By that time a group of onlookers had accumulated and someone yelled, "Get the manager!"

To Claudia's astonishment, none other than Carole Pedrotti appeared, asking, "What's going on here?" And noticing the man's uncovered face she said, "No matter what this is about, you, sir, need to put on your mask."

The clerk explained, "That's the argument, he refuses to wear one."

With a sudden smile the man repeated, "All I need is two things. I'll be in-and-out of here in a jiffy."

Carole was about to make a retort when she spotted Claudia. "Well, well," she exclaimed for all to hear, "if it isn't Lieutenant Campbell from the Monrovia City Police Department!" And she faced the detective directly and said, "You're the law enforcer. Go ahead and handle it."

Claudia was not pleased. She had planned to make a quick stop to get her items and then go home and cook her meal, for which she was already hungry. She did not want to deal with this in an official way, filing a report and all. She had to be careful about how to approach the situation, since she was out of her jurisdiction in Pasadena.

Yes, there existed a law to wear masks in public places but, so far, she had never had occasion to enforce that law. Also, regardless of being in Pasadena or Monrovia, she was a detective and would in general not be in charge of dealing with such matters. Yet, put on the spot, she had no choice but to comply.

She walked over to the man and asked, "What is the reason for your refusal to wear a mask?"

"I don't have one," he answered.

"Oh, that's all? Let's step outside for a minute and I'll make you an offer," she said and left her basket by the entrance as they exited.

Once out in the open she continued, "I have extra masks in my car. Wait here and I'll fetch you one."

With that minor problem out of the way, she returned to the store, paid for her groceries, and was thankful to get home in a matter of minutes.

***

An hour later, while enjoying her Italian dinner, the scene at the grocery store replayed itself in Claudia's mind. Seeing Carole Pedrotti at her place of work, and the Schadenfreude that had come over the woman's face as she shoved the problem into the detective's lap, suddenly opened up a whole new train of thought. She saw Carole in her element and the magnetism she seemed to have with men wasn't lost on the detective. The unmasked man appeared to melt when the manager showed up.

I've looked at Cecile's homicide, and consequently at that of the gardener's, from the wrong angle and I've got to turn it upside down, she told herself. An inkling of the truth had surfaced before, but I shrugged it off as impossible. Under certain circumstances it could in fact be possible. I have to proceed with caution, though. If not, I could botch the entire investigation.

She concluded, I need to do more research and contact several people once more.

CHAPTER 45

Jason called another Zoom meeting on Wednesday, October 21, this time for only the Basic Wrappers' board of directors.

He opened the session with, "I've put this board meeting off for as long as I could, but I'm sure you all realize that we have to make major decisions. Before we start, I need to let you know that mom's estate lawyer, Eduard Blyte, will have a meeting with us next Monday, October 26, with information about mom's will. So mark that date.

"Now to business: The first item on the agenda is to decide who will take over Mom's job as CEO. He looked over at Julie's square and said, "I doubt that you'll be up for the job, Sis. If it will be Jason or me, we'll have to hire an outsider as CFO or CIO. Let's all take time to think about this and vote on it at another meeting soon."

Darrell said, "We don't want outsiders as officers."

"Are you willing to take on two jobs, then?"

Darrell did not respond, so Jason continued, "As I said, we need to think this over carefully. Then we'll vote on it. Number two on the agenda are the masks. In honor of Mom's wishes, I suggest that we continue to give them away free of charge."

Darrell protested, "That is sentimental hogwash. Don't be a hypocrite, Jason! When she was alive, we all agreed that we needed to make a profit where masks are concerned or Basic Wrappers will not survive. Next, you'll tell us that we'll also take the 50 percent pay cut in her honor!"

His brother stated, "What happens with the masks will be voted on at our follow-up meeting. Until then, please keep your opinion about it to yourself. The reduction of our salaries was the next thing on my list. We may get away with a lesser cut. I will have the exact financial calculations at hand by next week. It does not look like the pandemic will end any time soon, so some percentage of a cutback is indicated. It also depends on how much personal money Mom leaves behind. Remember, she said that she'd chip in with her private assets, if necessary. We'll have a better picture after Eduard Blyte talks with us on Monday.

"We all know that orders from restaurants and hair salons haven't come our way as they used to. Like Mom mentioned at her last board meeting, we have to be creative and come up with products essential to the general public during the current crisis. I totally agree that we have to offer additional items in order to survive. Julie, have you thought about what extra merchandise we could add to the production line?"

Without warning, Julie let go of her pent-up emotions and shouted, "What's the matter with you two? Conducting business as usual when we have a murderer running loose among us! We look at each other full of suspicion and dread, not knowing who the culprit is. You're talking about who should succeed Mom as CEO when anyone of us may get arrested at any moment. I don't know about you, but my nerves are about to explode. My friends are avoiding me, wondering if I'm a killer. Even Basic Wrappers' employees are looking at me sideways."

She inhaled and went on, "And that woman detective is dragging her feet. It has been over a month since Mom was strangled to death and she hasn't solved the crime. And now poor Mr. Ibarra was murdered too, and God only knows who is next. It's obvious that the woman is incompetent. I suggest that we hire a private investigator."

Darrell said, "Calm down already, Julie. I doubt that employing a sleuth would speed things up."

Jason put in, "For now, we can't afford the extra expense anyway."

Darrell continued, "As for the rest of your tantrum, what makes you so sure the guilty person is one of us? Mom wasn't an open book where her private life was concerned. Heck, she even kept her illness a secret from us. She may have made enemies, for all we know, and one of them may have had reason to kill her."

"Stop being so melodramatic, both of you," Jason cried out. "This is a board of directors' business meeting and not some kind of family feud."

He nodded at the screen for emphasis and continued, "Yes, we're all on edge and anxious to learn the truth about both killings. I'm having sleepless nights about it too, but we have to think of what's best for the company. That should be our main goal right now, and that's the way Mom would handle it if she were in our shoes. I don't know the exact details of her will, but I do know that all three of us are inheriting Basic Wrappers and with that comes responsibility."

He ended the session with, "We will vote on the issues I've put on the table next week. Meeting adjourned."

CHAPTER 46

On Friday, October 23, exactly five weeks after Cecile's murder, Bruce answered the front doorbell to find Lieutenant Campbell and Sprint at his threshold.

"You come in person and bring an assistant, so you must have news for me," he said. And as he ushered them toward the study, he added, "I can't wait to learn what you've discovered. Can I offer you anything to drink?"

"No, thanks," the law officers replied in unison.

Campbell and Sprint seated themselves on the sofa and Bruce settled into an upholstered chair, facing them.

The detective said, "As I discussed with you a week ago at our Facetime session, I've focused on Raul Ibarra's homicide and have made real progress. Establishing Ibarra's killer led me to discover who strangled your wife."

"Tell me already, I can't take the suspense!"

"I'm getting there. Evidence shows that Mr. Ibarra's shed was set on fire a minute or two after 12 o'clock noon. Driving time from the gardener's residence in San Fernando to the Hansen Dam golf course is 12 minutes. And I verified the driving times you mentioned during our talk, namely that it was 30 minutes from Mr. Jason Long's house and 35 minutes from your house to get to that particular golf course.

"I also researched the driving times from each of your residences to the San Fernando location. And guess what? They are exactly the same: 30 and 35 minutes, respectively."

Bruce reflected on this and then said, "You mean, Jason drove to Ibarra's house first, set the shed on fire, and then drove to the golf course?"

"If we take Mr. Long and his wife's statements at face value, he left his house at noon and arrived at the golf course at 12:30, verified by you and the attendant. There was no time for a stop in-between."

"So what are you saying?"

"I turned the thing around and in that case, the evidence points to you, Mr. Horton."

Bruce nearly jumped out of his seat and roared, "That's absurd!" And after a moment he continued, "You stated just now that it takes 35 minutes to get from my house to San Fernando. I couldn't have driven there since I left here at 11:40 and got to Hansen Dam at 12:15. I have my pool guy as a witness at this end, and the golf course attendant at the other."

"Yes, Mr. Horton, that was one of the mistakes you made when talking with me the other day."

"What the devil do you mean?"

"I thought it was strange that you forced the bit on me about your pool maintenance person being able to verify that you left your house at that time. I did not ask you for the information."

Campbell went on, "Initially, your alibi was tight. The young man who tends to your pool stated that you left your house indeed at 11:40, but when more and more evidence pointed in your direction, I had another chat with the man. I asked if the time he had stated was according to his wristwatch, and he replied that he did not wear one."

She looked at her notes and said, "Here are the young man's own words as he followed up his statement, 'Mr. Horton mentioned that it was 11:40 as he left.'"

"Well, that's his word against mine."

"The other blunder you made was also during the same chat we had. When I informed you that the time Mr. Ibarra's shed went up in flames was shortly after 12:00 noon, you said something like, 'That clears Jason. If he came straight from home, he wouldn't have left his house before twelve to arrive at the golf course at 12:30.' You thought you were clever by killing two birds with one stone with that sentence. By pretending you wanted Jason cleared - - while in fact you tried to frame him - - and at the same time leave doubt in my mind as to when exactly he left his house.

"So you see, it backfired. I started to pay close attention to not only Jason's timing but your timing as well."

"All circumstantial and will never hold up in court! And what other evidence are you talking about?"

"There is a witness who saw you at Mr. Ibarra's driveway and shed at the appropriate time."

"Nonsense! What witness?"

"The neighbor's teenage son looked out of his window and spotted you in the act of leaving a canister in the shed. You and I both know that the canister in question was filled with gasoline."

"The kid is mistaken. It wasn't me."

Campbell looked at Sprint, then back at her suspect, and stated, "We can arrange for a lineup for the boy to pick you out of. In the meantime, a photo I took of all that were present at that first Zoom meeting we had would suffice."

Bruce's protest was getting weaker but he still clung to his denial and said, "You can't prove that I killed Cecile.

Not only do I have an airtight alibi in her case, but I have no motive whatsoever. And since the two crimes are obviously connected, you have no chance of linking me to either one."

"You are wrong. As to motive, it's a classic case of monetary gain. You knew that you were not mentioned in Cecile's will and consequently figured you were out of the woods. But you also knew that you were the beneficiary of her life insurance in the amount of $800,000. So far, you have not made a claim to the insurance company, figuring if you waited long enough, hopefully until after someone else was charged with the murders, no one would notice. That was clever of you. Also clever was the casual remark you made on the day I dropped by about the deed to your house being registered under both your names."

A smile escaped her as she added, "That was the same day that your girlfriend, Carole Pedrotti, also dropped in, but that's another story. She sure pulled at your strings, that lady did. The financial gain was in reality not the only motive; getting and keeping Carole Pedrotti was even the stronger one. The prenuptial agreement with Cecile prevented you from asking for a divorce.

"Now back to your mentioning the joint ownership of the house. You had me fooled at the time. Just like you had intended, the remark made me think, the man is honest about owning the house and must have nothing to hide. And when you informed me that you didn't know the estate lawyer's name nor the terms of your wife's will, I shrugged it off as Cecile Long-Horton being an extremely secretive woman. Later, when I learned that you were not one of the beneficiaries of her will, I assumed that was her reason for keeping you in the dark. That theory of mine was all wrong.

"Now I know that your wife discussed it with you, and that you both decided that an actual sum would serve you better than an inheritance that would be divided among her three children and yourself and may decrease in value by the time of her death. That's why she made the life insurance in your favor instead."

Bruce protested, "No matter what, you can't prove I strangled her. I was in the dentist's office at the time of the murder. I have three people to attest to that: the receptionist, the hygienist, and even the dentist stuck his head in to say hi when I sat in the chair."

Campbell stated, "I have new evidence to support a flaw in the timing of your first crime but am not going into that at present."

She looked over at Sprint again, who made a slight nod with his head.

As if on command, both Sprint and she got up from the sofa and stepped in front of Bruce while she announced, "We hereby arrest you, Mr. Bruce Horton, for the murders of Cecile Long-Horton and Raul Ibarra."

Bruce got up from his chair too and stated, "I want to talk with my lawyer."

"You may in due process," she replied while snapping the handcuffs over his wrists.

"Sprint, read him the Miranda rights, will you?"

"With pleasure," her colleague replied.

CHAPTER 47

Bruce hired several lawyers and the interrogation team of the Monrovia City Police Department decided to let him stew in his cell over the weekend before starting the official questioning first thing Monday morning.

The weather had finally turned cold. It was too chilly to have an outdoor restaurant meal, so Claudia and Sprint settled for a Facetime date on Sunday evening. They poured themselves a glass of wine in their respective homes and held them up to their computer screens in a toast before starting their conversation.

"Cheers!" Sprint proclaimed, "and to the *sharing* of a bottle next time."

"Hear, hear!"

They had been department colleagues for years, but knew little about one another as individuals. Their chat was at first personal and covered topics common to new relationships. For instance, they learned that both liked hiking, bowling, and Italian food but hated sushi. Each had a past and they dwelled a bit on that. But soon their focus turned to Bruce Horton's arrest and what led to it.

Sprint said, "I came along in case he'd give you trouble, but you really didn't need me."

"We hauled him in peacefully, that's a fact," she agreed.

"I have no idea how you arrived at your findings. Last time we spoke about your investigation was on that Saturday when we met for dinner. On that occasion you told me about Raul Ibarra's perishing in the fire set to his shed. You mentioned that the gardener must have known something incriminating and was silenced. Did you find out what that was?"

"I'm still in the dark about that and hope it will come out in the course of Horton's interrogation. Killing the gardener was Bruce's downfall. And the poor man may not even have been a threat to him. Whatever he knew or saw may have not registered, but Bruce couldn't ignore it and silenced him. By the same token, I would have never been able to arrest the killer for the murder of his wife, were it not for his second crime."

Sprint said, "Everything you threw at him during his arrest was news to me. Tell me how you arrived at the information that convinced you of his guilt."

"I may have to start at the beginning to give you a clear picture."

"Shoot!"

And so Claudia told the story from beginning to end.

"When I first interviewed Bruce Horton a few hours after his wife's strangulation, he looked and acted like the grieving spouse, but I noticed a couple of suspicious reactions on his part. First, his cellphone rang. He didn't answer it but was either annoyed or scared when he looked at who the caller was. I couldn't tell which. Then later, still during the course of the interview, the landline rang and went to voicemail. Before the answering machine's recording played, I saw definite fear in Horton's eyes. When it turned out to be a telemarketing call, he visibly relaxed. I jotted it down as nervous tension; after all, the man's wife had just been murdered.

"There were other indications that he had something to hide, especially after his girlfriend dropped by unexpectedly, and I left him no choice but to come clean about her. But overall, he gave an impression of innocence. He was a clever manipulator in many ways. When I asked him if there was anyone who had a grudge against his wife or may have felt threatened by her, he at first answered in the negative.

"Now, looking back, it's as if he willed me to ask the same question again. When I did, he reluctantly shared what he had overheard of the board of directors' Zoom meeting, or so I thought at the time. In reality it was a ploy. He wanted to tell it all to throw a motive for murder in the direction of Cecile's kids."

Sprint interrupted, "What did he overhear?"

"That there had been a heated dispute with Cecile as CEO of the company insisting that masks would stay free of charge; that all siblings should take a 50 percent cut in pay; and the bad apple threat she made that I told you about."

"What exactly was that apple thing again?"

"As best I remember, Horton quoted her as 'There is a bad apple among us.' But as far as the homicide investigation goes, the apple comment is irrelevant. Horton sprung it on me in order to leave me with even more of an impression that one of the siblings had a secret to protect at all cost. Needless to say that he succeeded for a while."

Claudia continued, "You and I both know that we tend to suspect spouses of murder victims first, since we know that nine times out of ten, they are the culprits. In this case,

I could not pin the crime on the husband, since it looked like he had an airtight alibi. The coroner had determined that Cecile's death occurred close to 9 o'clock but not before. Bruce Horton sat in the dentist chair at 9:00 a.m. on the morning of the murder, so by logic he could not have committed the crime.

"As to motive, at first glance it also looked like he had none. As far as I knew, he did not inherit upon Cecile's death. On the contrary, having her alive and as the main source of income was in his best interest, since he had been recently furloughed. I didn't know of the prenuptial agreement at the time, so if he wanted out of the marriage for Carole Pedrotti's sake, divorce was his best option, I thought."

She took another sip from her wine glass and went on, "Assuming that the victim's kids had the strongest motive - - for a brief moment I also considered Antonia Silva - - I suspected any one of the three siblings but had nothing concrete to back it up. After Raul Ibarra's homicide, I finally had a lead. There was a witness, even if he was not sure he could identify the person he saw, but - - -"

"Did you really take a photo of all the people at the Zoom meeting, from which the kid picked Horton as the culprit?"

"Of course not! That was pure bluff but it got me the result I wanted. He thinks he was identified."

She continued, "Anyhow, at first, the evidence pointed to Jason Long. It took only 12 minutes to drive from Mr. Ibarra's house in San Fernando to the Hansen Dam Golf Course. If he and his wife lied about the time he left their residence in Sierra Madre and he started from home earlier, he could have driven to San Fernando first, done his dirty work, and continued on to the golf course.

"Also, when I interviewed Mr. Long, he stated that Bruce was the one who called him and suggested they play a round of golf on that particular day and at that particular course. Later, when I talked with Bruce Horton, he claimed that it was the other way around. One of the two men was lying and I figured it must be Jason. After all, Horton had the pool guy to back up his statement of the exact time he left home, and in Long's case it was his wife, which I could not take at face value.

"So I considered Jason Long as being the guilty person for a while, but it wouldn't leave me any peace. I knew in the back of my mind that I was missing a crucial fact. It was not until after I ran into Carole Pedrotti in the Super Market one evening that a light bulb turned on in my brain and all the puzzle pieces aligned themselves.

"I figured it out that same evening. First off, the thing that had bothered me about Jason was the timing. It was all wrong. Even if he left his house earlier, the shed was put on fire shortly after 12 o'clock noon. And by the time the neighbor's boy rode away on his bike and the caller reported the fire at 12:08, the culprit was long gone. It took only 12 minutes to drive from the scene to the golf course, so that would put Jason there at around 12:15, not when he actually arrived at 12:30."

"Makes sense," said Sprint.

"So I turned it around and thought, if Bruce Horton left his house earlier than he claimed, he could have committed the crime around 12:02 or 12:03, and arrived at the golf course just like he said at 12:15. I thought him cunning enough to instigate the golf date with his stepson, giving himself an alibi and at the same time framing the other. I contacted the young man who attended the Horton pool once more, figuring that Bruce might have bribed him to lie about the time he left home. As it turned out, it was as simple as a statement from Bruce saying something like, 'Oh, it's already 11:40, I had better hurry to get out of here.'

"Earlier in the investigation I had reason to suspect Bruce. One example was the virtual meeting where I informed all concerned that, according to her doctor, Cecile had only a few more months to live. What I read on his face was not only surprise but an expression that conveyed, 'I could have spared myself the trouble.'"

Sprint said, "I remember you mentioned that to me during one of your 'unburdening sessions,' but you kept who it was a secret."

"I didn't want to commit, in case I was wrong. There were other instances where my instinct pointed to him, but since I could not physically put him at Cecile's doorstep at the right time, I shrugged them off as being in my imagination.

"So although I had established who was responsible for Mr. Ibarra's murder, it seemed impossible to connect him to Cecile's. And as I said, when I saw Carole Pedrotti in action at her grocery store, I suddenly thought it might be possible under certain circumstances, but I needed to make a few phone calls."

Sprint held up his nearly empty glass and remarked, "Now you're getting to the beef, I'll drink to that!" and downed the last few drops of his wine.

Claudia picked up her narrative and stated, "I first called Cecile's lawyer, Eduard Blyte, and learned a few things. After my prying, he enlightened me that, not only did his client and Bruce have a prenuptial agreement, but also that Cecile had set up a life insurance to benefit her husband. Mr. Blyte even acknowledged that the two had come to his office together some 10 years ago, that they had discussed the matter, and had decided that a life insurance for Bruce was the best way to go, rather than to add him to her will. Mr. Blyte even gave me the name of the insurance company." With a grin she added, "The man is a typical, cautious attorney. When I asked him why he did not inform me of all that the first time around, his astute answer was, 'Your only inquiry was about her will.'

"Next, I got in touch with that insurance company. I had to threaten them with obtaining a court order, but in the end got what I needed: namely, that Bruce Horton was the beneficiary of an $800,000 life insurance policy. They also grudgingly admitted that so far there had been no claim.

"My last and most important call was to the coroner. I asked him whether it was possible that Cecile Long-Horton could have been unconscious for a few minutes before she actually died. His reply was that, although rare, that scenario was possible."

"Wow!" Sprint cried out, "What made you think of that possibility?"

"I figured, since everything else fits and the only flaw in my theory was the time of death by approximately 10 minutes, there had to be a way to get around it. It was a long shot, but as you can see it sticks."

Sprint asked, "Do you think there is enough evidence for a conviction?"

She replied, "The formal interrogation will start tomorrow. If we're lucky, he'll confess. If not, we have enough to put him on trial, and then it's out of our hands."

CHAPTER 48

At the beginning of April, 2021, a jury found Bruce Horton guilty of both murders, and he was sentenced to life in prison without parole. By that time, most people had been vaccinated against Covid-19 and had started to envision a normal life and sighed with relief.

For Bruce, however, the harsh reality of spending the rest of his days behind bars sank in. Like many convicted felons, he wrote his memoir in prison. He did this foremost for himself to keep from going insane but, to his surprise, the book was well received. Folks in general seem to be interested in the mindset of a murderer. The memoir spanned over his entire lifetime and only the last chapter dealt with his crimes.

The following excerpt is from that final chapter:

During the decade I spent being married to Cecile, I enjoyed a happy, comfortable, and satisfying life. Cecile was a good-looking, vibrant, and generous woman, and despite our age difference, we were compatible. In my own way I even loved her. I saw a financially worry-free, enjoyable, early retirement in the near future. All that came to a halt when Carole re-entered my life.

From the moment I spotted her at the class reunion, clear across the room, I was hooked again. Carole attracted like a magnet and I could not resist. The affair lasted for several months until the pandemic hit. Since the population was on lockdown, I could no longer get away. Cecile worked from home and I soon was furloughed from my job, making it impossible to escape. Besides, Covid-19 had me scared.

Meanwhile, Carole got impatient, pressuring me to get a divorce. That was out of the question because of the prenuptial agreement. I depended on Cecile as my source of income and the assurance of a financially worry-free life.

The idea started to nag at me that it would be nice to get the life insurance money and permanently get Carole as well. It was only a daydream at that stage; husbands were always the prime suspects in homicides, and I knew that chances were slim I'd get away with it.

The daydream soon became a reality. When I overheard the intense arguments between Cecile and her kids, and she ended by threatening them with cutting their salaries and also accused one of them of being a bad apple - - whatever that meant - - I knew that all three siblings, and one in particular, had a motive for killing their mother. What a great opportunity, I thought, and came up with a perfect plan.

Strangling her at the front doorstep would implicate someone from outside of her household. The risk of doing it in broad daylight was minimal; the neighbors on either side had no clear view to the front door, and from the neighbor's house across the street it was blocked by a tree. I had a dental appointment at 9 o'clock that day and knew that a grocery delivery was due an hour later. Unfortunately, I had forgotten that it was also the gardener's day of the week to come, which turned out to be my downfall. I timed it so that I would arrive back from my appointment after Cecile's body was discovered by the grocery delivery person.

There were two times when I hesitated with going through with it. The first was when I met up with Carole in the park during my morning jog. On that day, I had decided to forget about getting rid of Cecile and planned to break up with Carole instead. But when I came face to face with Carole, my good intentions blew in the wind and her strong hold on me won. It goes without saying that I could not let Carole in on my plan. Much too dangerous! But I needed to stay away from her in the near future, in order for my blueprint to work.

The other was when Cecile opened the front door to me on her fateful day, saying, "Oh, it's you!" in her most trusting way. I hesitated for a split second, wondering if I should go through with it. But then I placed my hands around her skinny neck and squeezed.

It worked like a charm and I thought that I had gotten away with it. There was a woman detective in charge of the investigation - - I will not mention her name - - and at first she did not seem all that competent to me. As expected, she concentrated on Cecile's kids, which made me believe that I was home free. After all, they were the ones with the motive and I had none, for all she knew. Later, I came to realize that I had underestimated her and needed to be on my guard.

The biggest blow came during a Zoom meeting when the detective informed us all that Cecile had been terminally ill with only a short time to live. What an ironic fluke nature had dealt me, I mused. If only I'd have waited a few months, my problem would have solved itself without me lifting a finger. At the same moment I had the feeling that the detective was staring at me and hoped my thoughts would not show.

My strategy was to wait until I was no longer being watched before making a claim to the insurance company. I might have even sold the house to tide me over until I was ready to claim the $800,000. I also needed to wait until an appropriate 'mourning' time had passed before I planned to hook up with Carole. I had it all figured out but by a twist of fate, all my careful planning had gone down the drain.

As I hinted at before, the gardener - - I am not revealing his name either - - turned out to be my ruin. He came up to me after everyone else had left on the day of the funeral and mentioned that he had been near my property earlier, before 9 o'clock, on the day of Cecile's murder. Apparently he had forgotten some tool and needed to drive back to his place to fetch it before returning to my residence. His wording was clumsy when he tried to explain what he saw the first time around, but I understood. During the brief moment he was stationary at the curb in his truck before making a U-turn, he noticed that I came out of the side door and walked around to the front, where I rang my own doorbell.

He said that at the time he didn't give the matter a thought but later, when remembering it, he realized that it was strange. If I needed to go back in, why wouldn't I use the side door where I had come out of, he asked. The thing didn't leave him any peace, but he was sure I could explain. At first, I thought that the man tried to blackmail me. When he did not make any move in that direction but looked at me expecting an answer, I had to come up with something quick.

I stated, "I forgot my sunglasses; they were sitting inside the front entrance." He seemed to take my explanation at face value and said, "Thank you, Mr. Horton, I won't have to worry about it no more."

I may have satisfied his curiosity for a while, but I could not be sure that he would not think about it later, wondering why I would have needed to ring the doorbell to my own house. No, I could not take any chances and needed to come up with a plan to eliminate him. I was lucky the man did not stick around on his first run to witness what happened after Cecile opened the door.

Also by a stroke of luck, the man had mentioned earlier, as everyone was gathered in my backyard, that he needed to find someone who would be interested in buying his bronze collection. The gardener was the last to leave my property, and as he was doing so, I told him I was interested in his bronzes and that I would like to have a look at them someday soon.

Up until plotting my second crime, I had no preference for which of Cecile's kids would be the scapegoat in her murder. Any one of them would do. When planning the killing of the gardener, though, I wanted to frame someone and at the same time establish my own alibi. I thought of the golf idea, with the Hansen Dam course being so close to the gardener's home in San Fernando. Both Jason and Derrell played golf and I mulled over which one to pick as the stooge. Jason won. He appeared to be a nervous wreck - - might have been the pandemic or some other issue - - but whatever the cause, it could work to my advantage, I decided.

I had timed the torching of the gardener's shed to perfection, or so I believed. The day before, I talked Jason into playing golf at Hansen Dam and said I would make a reservation for the next day and call him back with the tee time. Then I got in touch with the gardener and told him I could have a look at his bronze collection on the next day. That suited the man fine as he planned to come home for lunch. We arranged to meet at his house at noon.

So I got there early and set the stage, so to speak. Walking down his driveway and pouring gasoline all over the inside of the shed was accomplished in no time. When the gardener arrived in his truck, I was waiting for him in front of the house. Getting him to enter the shed, throwing in a lighted book of matches, and jamming the door from the outside was child's play. I reached the Hansen Dam Golf Course at 12:15, fifteen minutes before tee time. I had told Jason that tee time was at 12:45, so he got there late at 12:30.

I had wanted Jason to arrive late so that it would be construed he stopped in San Fernando first to commit the crime before getting to the golf course. But it backfired. I had not taken into account that the driving time from the first place to the next was only 12 minutes. The clever woman detective did, however. She also claimed that there was an eyewitness to my torching of the shed, but that's another story.

Was it worth the risk? No way! I exchanged a perfectly comfortable life for this miserable rat hole I am stuck with now forever. What was I thinking? Carole, for whom I gave up everything I had and a worriless future, has moved on and is not even visiting me in prison. As far as she is concerned, I am a total loser.

I wonder if she would have stuck with me had I gotten away with the crimes. I was so obsessed with her at the time. Funny, now I hardly ever think of her. Cecile, on the other hand, is always on my mind.

EPILOGUE

Basic Wrappers survived the Coronavirus pandemic. In fact, business was booming. Orders resumed from the company's established clientele of restaurants and beauty salons after government restrictions were lifted. In addition, Basic Wrappers created a new line to supply hospitals with gowns. Soon, the demand for those hospital gowns kept the sewing machines rattling non-stop at the El Monte plant.

Since the siblings inherited the company equally, each became a partner. For a while, Jason tried to keep up with both jobs, that of CEO and CFO, but soon became overwhelmed. He was best educated and suited to tending to the finances of the company, so he carried on as CFO and hired a qualified outsider as CEO, who was an employee without a chance of becoming a partner. Even Darrell had to admit that this was the best solution.

As to people's private lives, Jason did seek help with his opioid addiction. He went through a period of tough times, first with individual counseling, followed by group therapy. Candy helped him through it all with patience and understanding. In the end, she got her loving husband back, and Mike and Sophia got a daddy who took an interest in them again.

As promised, Julie quit her phone sex hobby on the day Mateo found her extra cellphone. She returned the offensive phone together with the fantasy name Brigitte. Whether or not someone would take over her role was something she did not lose sleep over. Gradually her husband forgave her and their relationship returned to being harmonious.

For her penance Julie purchased a stationary bicycle and had it installed along the hallway on the second floor of the El Monte plant. Now she passed part of her lunchbreaks exercising on it. On many such occasions she envisioned her mom and maintained thoughts like, "I'm doing this for you and hope you can see me," or "I'm sorry I said that I hated you. I didn't mean it," and finally, "Rest in peace, Mom!"

Darrell never shaped up where his gambling was concerned. On the contrary, his addiction got even worse. Sybille urged him numerous times to get help, but he always found an excuse to put if off for later. The day came when she followed through with her warning of no longer being able to stand by him. She served him divorce papers, before he got a chance to gamble his inheritance away. Unlike with her mother-in-law and Bruce, there was no prenuptial agreement between Darrell and Sybille. She made out like a bandit.

Antonia Silva put the main portion of her legacy inheritance into a college fund for her kids. She did allow herself one luxury, however: a brand-new SUV, paid for in cash. Besides having a car of her own to drive to her housekeeping jobs and chauffeuring the kids - - until now she and her husband had shared one - - Antonia used it for a special ritual.

Once a month, she drove to the Forest Lawn Cemetery in Arcadia and placed flowers at the plaque beneath which Cecile Long-Horton's ashes were buried, bowing her head and saying, "Thank you, good lady."

The irony of this story is that Cecile took the secret of who she meant by being a bad apple - - and why - - all the way to her grave and beyond.

Stand-Alone Mysteries by Alice Zogg
A Bad Apple
Exposing the Past
No Curtain Call
The Ill-Fated Scientist
Accidental Eyewitness
A Bet Turned Deadly

R. A. Huber Mysteries by Alice Zogg
Evil at Shore Haven
Guilty or Not
Murder at the Cubbyhole
Revamp Camp
Final Stop Albuquerque
The Fall of Optimum House
The Lonesome Autocrat
Tracking Backward
Turn the Joker Around
Reaching Checkmate